BE MINE, VALENTINE

A HOLIDAY ROMANCE NOVELLA

DANIELLE BAKER

ISBN #979-8-9880456-6-3

Formatting: Books From Beyond

This is for all the girls that never
stopped reading fairytales...
They're just spicier, now.

Beau is waiting for you, besties.

CHAPTER 1

"*R*omance is dead, and so is chivalry."

Valentina Compton watched as her sister rolled her eyes, sighing heavily at her. She stomped her way around the small stock room of their flower shop, *Three Blossom Haven*.

"He bought *two bouquets*," she grated out, rounding on Noelle. "And we're just supposed to ignore the fact that one is for his wife and the other is for his secretary?"

"*Val*," Noelle groaned, setting the floral scissors down with a metallic thunk on the counter in front of her. "Calvin Jons has bought two bouquets every Valentine's Day for the last ten years. His secretary is twenty years his senior and he and his wife just celebrated their seventeenth wedding anniversary."

"I don't need you to use logic on me, Noelle," she snapped, stomping over to the giant wall of refrigerated coolers that housed thousands of florals. Grabbing out a dozen red roses and a handful of bright pink peonies, she brought them back over to the counter, standing opposite her sister. "I still think it's suspicious."

Rolling her eyes again, Noelle went back to arranging a

bouquet of deep red, blush pink, and white roses, gathering them together with sprigs of baby's breath and eucalyptus.

"Just because you're on a man hating journey doesn't make every man a douche bag," she muttered, giving her a side eye as they worked. Noelle's dark hair was pulled up into a high, messy topknot, an elastic headband keeping her flyaways away from her face. Purple shadows rimmed her dark green eyes, a testament to the little sleep she'd gotten the night before. Neither one of them had slept more than a couple hours. Her own eyes felt gritty from lack of sleep... and crying.

"Yeah, well, I'm not in a very generous mood right now," Val mumbled bitterly, slicing into the peonies. The soft tinkling of a bell could be heard from the front, as a new customer walked in.

Noelle reached out her hand and covered hers, stilling her hand. She squeezed gently, which made Val raise her eyes to hers finally. "It's his loss, you know that right?"

Val rolled her eyes. "Don't start with the 'he didn't deserve you' and 'he didn't know what he had' bullshit, please. Right now, I just want to wallow in self-pity at being dumped the night before Valentine's Day and hate on every single man that walks through those doors to buy flowers and chocolates. Can you let me have that, please?"

"Okay, but just back here. I expect to see a big ol smile on your face if you're in front of a customer. Got it?" Noelle said sternly, but a smile tugged at her mouth. "As soon as they walk back out the door, you're welcome to do all the man hating your little heart can hold."

"Deal."

Val turned as their youngest sister, Willow, breezed through the stock room door from the front, heading for the cooler. Her long blonde hair fell over her shoulder as she leaned down to peer into the glass door, a large red satin bow tied up where her hair was pulled into a half ponytail in celebration of the holiday. Valentine's Day was usually Val's favorite day of the year; how could it not be her favorite with a name like *Valentina*, but today seemed like a cosmic slap in the face. "Is Ethan Harris' bouquet ready? He's here."

Val pointed with the scissors toward one side of the giant cooler. "Second shelf, third on the right. The blue butterfly orchid." Spinning around, she checked the list behind her, then called over her shoulder, "And he gets a chocolate covered strawberry bouquet, too."

"Got it!" Willow called back as she breezed back toward the front, the gorgeous blue orchid in her hands. They could hear her from the front, her voice carrying as she laughed and spoke with the customer at the counter.

Val looked around the stock room, filled to the brim with all things Valentine's Day. Helium filled heart balloons, thousands of roses in every shade of pink and red imaginable. Along the other wall, an assortment of glass and crystal vases were stacked on shelves. She and her sisters had inherited the small-town flower shop from their Aunt Jackie when she retired the year before and had rebranded it to represent the three sisters. This was their first Valentine's Day as the new owners. Anxiety over failing in their first big holiday had kept Val awake for two days straight... and the fact she'd been dumped the night before.

Thank the lord for triple espressos.

The bell tinkled again, followed by another jingle seconds later, and a male voice called through the stock room door, "Ladies! I come bearing gifts!"

And thank the lord for longtime family friends coming in clutch with coffee and muffins from the coffee shop next door.

Theo Collins strolled through the stockroom door, a recyclable drink carrier in one hand laden with cups of coffee, and a brown paper sack in the other. Stepping forward, he set both on the counter between herself and Noelle with a flourish.

"Beau sent me over with these, said he saw your light on at about two this morning," he said and smiled at her.

"Your brother is a saint," Val sighed with a smile and plucked the coffee with a V on the lid, taking a deep swallow of the triple espresso Americano. "I'm so tired I could sleep for a week. Tell him thank you for us."

Theo stood next to Noelle, their shoulders almost touching. He was tall and thin, built like a basketball player with long legs and narrow hips encased in jeans. Strong shoulders were hidden beneath a red and blue flannel shirt and a quilted gray vest that was left open. A gray ball cap covered his blonde head, the long ends sticking out from the bottom where they curled at his nape.

The Compton's and the Collins' had grown up next door to each other. Beau was the oldest at thirty-nine, several years older than herself, with her thirty-third birthday in two weeks. Theo and Noelle stuck in the middle, both twenty-nine, with Willow bringing up the caboose as the youngest at twenty-four. Theo and Noelle had been in the same class since kindergarten.

"You know he's going to send over lunch later if you three don't take a break by this afternoon," he said, picking up a sprig of baby's breath and rolling it between his fingers before Noelle snatched it out of his hand. He flicked the end of her nose, and she stuck her tongue out at him. "Don't make him go all 'big brother' on you girls."

"I promise we will head over for lunch," Noelle promised.

"I'm not hungry."

Theo pinned her with a stare. "That sounded more like 'I'd rather gargle shards of glass' than a simple 'I'm not hungry.'"

Val shrugged, taking another drink of her coffee.

"What happened?" Theo asked, his blue eyes bouncing from her to Noelle and back.

"Ryan broke up with her last night," Noelle explained, cutting off the tirade that was on the tip of her own tongue. She clicked her teeth shut and lowered her eyes to the florals in her hands. "She's on a man hating binge today."

4

Leaning on his forearms on the counter, he ducked his head down to catch her gaze. "That true, Val?"

"I don't know that we can even call it being dumped. We were only casually dating for a couple months. Dating after divorce is its own special kind of hell," Val added on a mumble, turning to place the peony and rose bouquet in a vase. She reached for a strip of white satin ribbon and tied it around the vase in an artful bow. "Your brother said Ryan was a waste of time. I didn't listen."

"Well, yeah, there's that," Theo laughed gently, his hands gesturing in front of him where he was still leaning against the counter. "I won't tell Beau he was right though. It'll go straight to his head, and his ego is already out of control."

"Go back to work, Theo, and leave me to my wallowing. I'll never hear the end of it if you tell Beau about this," she muttered, though a hint of a smile tugged at one corner of her lips.

He grinned widely, his smile dazzling. "You can have today, Grumpy Pants."

"Get out of here, we've got work to do," Val laughed, waving him off with the scissors still in her hand. "Tell your brother we will be over for lunch."

Theo pushed himself up off his forearms and winked at her. "You know he'll come over here if you don't."

When he had disappeared through the door and they heard the telltale tinkle of the bell as he left, Val leaned on her elbows across the counter and whined, "I really don't want to go to lunch today. Can I please just stay here and pretend nothing out there exists?"

"Absolutely not, because I don't need big burly Beau freaking Collins coming in here like a damn bull in a China shop pissed off because you refused to put anything in your body other than four triple espressos," Noelle snapped, though her eyes softened. "You know he takes that promise seriously."

Val nodded, her nose stinging with tears at the memory, but pushed it aside, not ready or willing to let the grief wash over her again. Not today, at least not right now. There was too much work to be done. This was their busiest day of the year, after all. Second only to Mother's Day.

"Ugh. Fine. You're a pain in my ass, you know that?" Val groaned, dropping her shoulders.

"Middle child," she mumbled around a bite of a chocolate chip muffin, pointing to her own chest. "It's in the job description."

CHAPTER 2

At quarter to one, Willow and Noelle finally begged for mercy, stating they were starving and couldn't work under these unfair conditions—never mind that they had both eaten two muffin's a piece—so Val taped a sign to the front door that read 'Out For Lunch. We Will Be Back in Fifteen Minutes'.

Willow then crossed out the 'Fifteen' and wrote a giant '30' across the page, which made Val roll her eyes. Noelle locked the door and the three of them hurried down the snow-covered brick sidewalk to *Beau's*. Mid-February in northern Michigan meant snow. Still. Lots and lots of snow.

The wide glass windows that lined the front of *Beau's* were frosted from the cold, and when they whisked their way through the door the heat was welcome after the chill from outside.

A long, wide counter ran the length of the back of the room. Polished concrete floors, red brick walls, and a black painted ceiling made the space striking aesthetically. The black metal and wood topped tables dotted around the center of the room were filled with customers, as were the black leather booths along the far side of the room. They passed a row of bar height tables with round stools, most of the seats occupied. Two plush black leather

9

sofas faced each other with a low wooden coffee table between them in front of the front windows. Patio lights were strung from the ceiling, casting everything in a warm glow.

The three of them stepped forward up to the counter, where Theo stood, typing into a touch screen tablet suspended on a stand. He grinned as they stepped up. "About time you all showed up. Beau stepped out for a few, so y'all are stuck with me. The usual, Noelle?"

"Actually, I just want a bowl of the beef barley soup and extra bread," she said, pulling open her purse. "And a giant cup of coffee with—"

"Hazelnut, yes I know," he laughed, tapping away on the screen. He turned to Willow, who smiled and opened her mouth, but he said, "Blackened Chicken Sandwich, extra avocado, no bacon."

She nodded, laughing. "You and Beau are mind readers, I swear. May I get the Valentine's White-Hot Chocolate with extra whipped cream and heart sprinkles, please?"

"Extra whip and extra sprinkles, you got it," he chuckled, then turned to Val, leaning on the counter. "I know what you would normally get today. But since we're man hating, what are we switching to? And I've been instructed that you don't get any more espresso, no matter how much you beg. Sorry."

Val rolled her eyes. "Fine. May I please have a regular coffee with French vanilla, whip, and a dash of cinnamon? And I'll take the Caesar salad, please."

"Extra Parmesan?"

"You know it," she laughed as he tapped the screen. Noelle passed him her credit card, but he waved her off, despite their protests. Val stuck a twenty-dollar bill in the tip jar before they wandered off to find an empty table.

They found a booth along the far side of the room toward the back. Willow and Noelle slid into one side of the booth, Val on the other. Classic Slow Rock music drifted to them over the speakers embedded in the ceiling and in the corners of the room, loud enough to hear over the din of voices, but quiet enough to still be able to hold a conversation without shouting. It wasn't long before their names were called out, and Willow slid out of the booth to grab their drinks, coming back with two mugs of coffee and a sugary confection with red and pink heart sprinkles all over the mountain of whipped cream on top. A paper straw with pink hearts was stuck into the whipped cream.

Val took her coffee with a normal amount of whipped cream floating on top dusted with cinnamon, brought it to her lips, and took a sip. It was hot and delicious. They were chatting about the orders that had already gone out that morning, and others that were still waiting to go out for the afternoon delivery when Theo showed up at their table bearing a small black tray laden with food. He set Val's salad down in front of her, then Willow's sandwich, and finally Noelle's soup with extra bread, the end pieces they cut off their house made bread loaves.

He scooted into the seat next to Val, picking up one of the chunks of bread and dipping it into Noelle's soup, then popped it into his mouth. She swatted his hand away with a shocked, "Hey!"

But he just grinned. "Quality check. Had to make sure it wasn't poisoned."

"You're a menace!" Noelle laughed, shaking her head. "Do you quality check all of your customers' food? Because I'm pretty sure that's a health code violation."

"Of course not!" he exclaimed, looking affronted. "I don't care if the rest of them get poisoned."

"You have customers, go away!" Noelle said, rolling her eyes. He grinned and stood, retreating to his spot behind the counter.

Val leaned her elbows on the table and whispered loudly, "That boy has been in love with you for as long as I can remember. Please tell me you see that, right?"

"What? Eww," Noelle muttered, shaking her head. "You're

11

insane. And it's *Theo*. He used to pick his boogers and wipe them on me."

"Noelle, he was like five! *You* used to lick all of Marnie's cookies so he couldn't have any!"

Noelle shrugged, grinning. "He used to get so mad that I put my 'cooties' on everything."

"Didn't he step in as your senior prom date when Matt Hinnum stood you up?" Willow asked around a bite of her sandwich.

"Oh my god, I totally forgot about that," Noelle said, nodding. She picked up a chunk of the bread on her plate, dipping it into her soup. "He was on crutches from that soccer injury, too. He still managed to dance with me." She shrugged then. "He's just a friend, you guys know that. Marnie and Mom have always been close, Dad and Drew were best friends... And we were always stuck together for everything in school because our last names are both C's. He's not in love with me." Waving her spoon in Val's face, Noelle continued, "It's you and your obsession with all things *love*. I'm not going to lie, it's kind of a nice break from your usual over-the-top insanity with this damn holiday. It's like you only see the world through rose-colored glasses all the time and you think that there's a Hallmark love story romance waiting around every corner. You read too many smutty romances."

Willow nodded in agreement next to Noelle. "I support that statement."

"There is nothing wrong with a good smutty romance novel, thank you very much," Val protested, laughing, as she stabbed a crouton with her fork. "I have been on five hellish first dates, two even worse second dates, and then whatever these last two months have been with Ryan." Taking a bite of her salad, she chewed and swallowed before she said, "So if I want to immerse myself in a good ol smutty romance novel and imagine that some totally ripped, outrageously handsome, heavily tattooed lumber-jack of a man with a thick beard is going to stroll his way into my flower shop one day, sweep me off my feet and give me a dozen orgasms, that is my prerogative!"

"Oh, come on now, a woman like you deserves at least two dozen orgasms, Val," a deep voice murmured from behind her and she jumped, dropping her fork with a clatter.

CHAPTER 3

⸎

*T*he deep flush of red that tinged her cheeks and made
her face feel like it was on fire caused him to chuckle,
the bastard.

"Beau!" Val stuttered, laughing, as she slapped her palms to
her cheeks. The waves of her dark hair swished around her
shoulders, the ends brushing her collarbone as she shook her
head. "You were *not* supposed to hear that!" Turning to glare at
her sisters, she hissed, "You could have told me he was right
behind me!"

Her sisters laughed, and he chuckled lightly. She watched as
he snagged one of the black metal-backed chairs from a nearby
table and dragged it to the end of their booth, straddling it back-
ward. His well worn, faded blue jeans pulled taut over muscled
thighs that were spread wide around the back of the chair. Black
work boots covered his feet. A blue flannel shirt was left unbuttoned over a black t-shirt that fit snug to his body, and the arms
of the flannel were pushed up his forearms, revealing the tattoos
that covered them.

He pushed the fingers of one hand up through thick black
hair that was fashionably too long and streaked with silver,

shoving the thick strands back away from his forehead. A dark beard trimmed about an inch long covered the lower half of his face and upper lip, also streaked through with threads of silver. The man had started graying in his early thirties and it only made him that much more attractive. Impossibly dark, chocolate brown eyes fringed with thick, dark lashes were focused on her face. The grumpy façade was a damn chick magnet, and he knew it, too. His body was thick all over, but muscle rippled under his skin. He was big and burly cantankerous, and when he fixed that impenetrable glare on someone, more than slightly intimidating.

God, I love a dad-bod, she thought wistfully, then rolled her lips inward and blinked rapidly to dispel the thought.

Folding his tattooed arms across the back of the chair, he leaned close and murmured, "So I heard Ryan proved me right."

"*Ugh, that little shit*," Val muttered sourly, turning to give Theo a dark glare from across the room. "He wasn't supposed to tell you that."

Glancing over at Beau again, she dropped her gaze to her food to avoid his eyes. She hated that stare that he leveled on her, the one that could see everything, even the parts that she didn't want anyone else to see. It was like his own annoying superpower.

"We're man hating today," Noelle informed Beau with a smirk. "No one is off limits, even you. But thank you for our lunches."

Beau chuckled again, a small smile tilting up one corner of his mouth. He had straight white teeth and an impossibly full bottom lip. Val had admittedly had a crush on Beau as a teen, but the man was as closed off emotionally as the brick wall they were sitting against. She'd never known the man to date more than for casual hookups. He was a self-proclaimed, lifelong bachelor. He lived in an apartment above the coffee shop that she knew was decorated similarly to the shop itself. Brick walls, old fashioned hardwood floors, black furniture, minimal décor and heaven forbid there be any *feminine touches* in his space. Women were not invited to stay overnight, and as far as Val knew, she and her sisters were the only women outside of his immediate family or casual hookups to be invited in at all.

She knew he had dated while he was away at college, but upon returning home to northern Michigan, he'd been single. He was single-handedly responsible for breaking a dozen mama's hearts because he had no interest in settling down or marrying their daughters.

Beau Collins was like an all-black, ten-thousand-piece puzzle with odd shapes as the pieces. It would take a miracle to ever figure out this man. He was polite, cordial, and always willing to help in any capacity... but he liked his privacy and didn't let anyone in.

"Do I need to be worried about you ladies for dinner tonight, as well?" he asked, his deep voice gruff.

"Oh lord, no," Willow laughed, setting her sandwich down. "Noe and I have dates tonight."

"I'll be home with a bottle of wine or a pint of ice cream, and possibly a slasher movie," Val said on a chuckle, only half joking. "Guess it was pointless for me to buy that new dress for tonight."

"Put it on and wear it around the house!" Noelle said then. "You get dressed up for *you*, not some douchey guy."

"Was Ryan supposed to take you out tonight?" Beau asked, pinning her with that dark stare again.

She shook her head, shrugging her shoulders in a non-committing gesture. "I mean, we'd talked about a date tonight, but I don't even care about that—"

"I'll do it."

Val's words halted and she stared over at him. "What?"

He shrugged those impossibly wide shoulders, the muscles under the flannel shifting with the movement. "I'll take you out tonight."

Val laughed nervously then, glancing at her sisters in shock. "Beau, you don't want to take me out for a date, especially on Valentine's Day—"

"Don't tell me what I want or don't want, Valentina," he rumbled darkly, his dark brows pulling low over his eyes. "I'll pick you up at seven."

"Look, *Beauregard*—" Val snapped sourly, using his full name since he'd used hers. She crossed her arms over her chest and glared over at him, muttering, "—I appreciate that you feel this responsibility to take care of us since our dad died but taking me on a Valentine's date because I got dumped is not part of your job description. And I don't need your pity date!"

Beau's eyes darkened and he leaned over the back of the chair until he was less than a foot away. "Responsibility be damned. I'm giving you an excuse to put on whatever sexy dress you want to and flaunt yourself all over this small town, because it will get back to Ryan within two hours what an idiot he was to let you slip through his fingers. He is not worth the bottle of wine or pint of Cherry Garcia you would consume tonight at home by yourself, or the nightmares you'll have tonight if you watched a scary movie alone. I've never once taken a woman out for Valentine's... so if I didn't want to, trust me, I wouldn't. *Val.*"

He stood, swinging his leg from the chair. He lifted it by the back and set it back down at the table he'd pulled it from earlier and then turned toward them, leaning his hands on the smooth wooden top of their booth table.

"I'll pick you up at seven."

And then he was gone, disappearing behind the counter as a group of teenagers stepped up to order.

Val stared at him for a long time, lunch forgotten, when Willow leaned over and whispered, "It's probably because I just binge watched all the seasons of *Riverdale*, but does he not remind either of you of *Skeet Ulrich*?"

CHAPTER 4

*B*eau Collins watched as the Compton women finished their meals. When they were finished, they brought their dishes to the far side of the counter where his dishwasher Jimmy took them to the back to wash. Noelle and Willow waved as they crossed the polished concrete floor to the door, but Val stopped at the door, looking back at him for just a heartbeat before slipping out into the cold. Through the frosted window, he watched as she hunched her shoulders against the bitterly cold February wind, rushing down the sidewalk toward *Three Blossom*.

He wasn't entirely sure what had prompted him to make his offer. He hated everything about this damn holiday; hated all the idiotic, societal bullshit about dating in general.

If it was up to him, he'd completely ignore the stupid candy-store-Hallmark holiday. But specialty holiday themed drinks always brought in more customers, even though he'd rather gargle a hand grenade than dust another hot chocolate with pink and red heart sprinkles.

Aside from the promise he'd made to their father just before he'd died, there had always been something in Val that tugged at him. To see her so despondent, today of all days, wrenched at his heart.

Valentine's Day had always been Val's Christmas. Even as a kid she'd saved up all her chore money and purchased carnations from her Aunt Jackie to hand out to her classmates, her family, her teachers. She'd always handmake elaborate Valentine's Day cards for everyone she could think of. Shit, last year, he'd received a handmade, quilled card—which he'd been informed is the art of rolling tiny bits of paper into elaborate designs—with beautiful hand drawn calligraphy. All that read on the inside was, *'Roses are red, violets are blue, you were right, boys suck'* in that fancy calligraphy. He'd laughed out loud upon opening it and reading it, but his heart had ached, as it was so unlike her.

He'd immediately picked up the phone and called her. She'd answered, her voice wobbling, and then she'd burst into tears. He'd let her cry, and when she'd calmed enough to talk, she told him she and her husband of six years were divorcing, and she hadn't even told her family yet. A month later, he and Theo, along with Noelle and Willow, had arrived in front of her house with a pickup truck and a U-Haul, and brought her home to Northern Michigan.

He lived in a studio apartment above his coffee shop, and at the top of the stairs there was a small landing. To the left was his apartment, and to the right, a mirror image studio apartment he'd previously been renting out to a college kid. The kid had moved out two weeks prior, and he'd insisted that Val move into it after she'd expressed how mortified she was at having to move back home after a failed marriage at the age of thirty-two.

With Val returning home and Willow just graduating from college, their Aunt Jackie had decided it was high time she retired and handed over the floral shop to the three girls, happily moving herself to Florida to escape the bitterly cold Michigan winters.

Val had seemed to come back into herself upon taking over

the floral shop with her sisters. She was thriving on her own... until the girl with permanent hearts in her eyes had decided to try dating four months ago.

She's such a damn bleeding heart, he thought ruefully with a shake of his head as he wiped down a newly deserted table. Noelle was tougher, not as easily taken advantage of, and Willow... well, she was simply a stick of dynamite waiting to go off. He rarely worried about those two. But Val... she was kind, sensitive, soft, and so easily heartbroken.

And those damn books she always reads don't help, he thought grumpily, as he prepared a caramel latte for a customer. *How was any normal man supposed to measure up to a six foot seven, winged fae warrior with a schlong the size of a salami capable of doling out a dozen orgasms?*

Not that he would ever admit to having read *those* books... or any of the other books she'd become captivated with in the last year. But he also stayed up to date with the TV shows that Willow liked best, even if he wanted to gouge out his eyeballs and rupture his eardrums afterwards. He had made sure to watch every *University of Michigan* football game with Noelle—while obstinately wearing his alma mater *Michigan State University* hoodie just to rile her up. And every Wednesday he would take their mother Rachel out for dinner.

All small sacrifices toward his promise to Hank.

The afternoon flew by in a flurry of snow, gaggles of tween girls looking for the Valentine's White-Hot Chocolate, and Willow, who snuck over for another round of coffee's around four that afternoon. He raised an eyebrow and shook his head when she requested a triple espresso. He crossed his arms over his chest.

"She's not getting any more espresso," he muttered darkly. "She's going to vibrate out of her skin or stop her heart."

The little devil even tried to deny that it was for Val. She'd finally given up and ordered regular coffees for all three of them and slunk back to the flower shop next door, with a request from him that she ascertained that she would do. Secretly.

At five thirty, he nodded to Miles, his second shift supervisor and called good-byes to the remaining customers before slinging his black leather jacket on and pushing out the door into the February cold.

He could still see the lights on in *Three Blossom*, illuminating the sidewalk to his left, so he made the short walk over to their windows and peered inside. The door was locked, their sign flipped to *closed*, but through the doorway in the back he could see Val hunched over her laptop. She reached out and took a drink of likely stone-cold coffee out of a disposable cup before she scrubbed her other hand over her face wearily.

He jogged back toward the coffee shop, pulling the door open and striding inside. Theo sat at one of the black leather sofas and tilted his head slightly at the sight of him back already, but didn't say anything. Beau rounded the counter and poured a fresh cup of coffee—decaf, this time—and added a dash of French vanilla, then topped it with whipped cream before lidding it. He waved another quick farewell and pulled his phone out of his jeans pocket.

He made it back to the glass door of the flower shop when she answered.

"Are you bailing on me already, Collins?" she drawled, and he watched her glance at the clock.

"Come open the door," he rumbled, his voice thick. When her eyes snapped toward the door and saw him standing there on the other side of it, he raised the coffee cup in his right hand. "Come on. That coffee you're sipping on has to be stone cold. I have a fresh one for you. Not that you need any more fucking caffeine today."

He watched her roll her eyes, but she stood from the little stool she was perched on and came toward the door. She hung up the call and he slid his phone back in his pocket as she reached the door, unlocking it and pulling it open to let him inside.

"You're my hero, on more than one account, today," she teased lightly, closing her hands around the disposable cup, her fingers grazing his. "Thank you, Beau."

He notched his head toward the back room. "Is there anything else you need to do tonight? Let your mind rest a little. Go on upstairs and take a hot shower, unwind from the day. I'm still picking you up at seven."

She rolled her eyes again. "You make it sound like you're traveling halfway across the city instead of across the hallway," she teased again, lifting the coffee to her lips. "Although a hot shower does sound heavenly right now. Two am came early this morning."

He plucked the coffee out of her hands, setting it aside, and then turned her by placing his hands on her shoulders. "Go get your stuff. I'll walk you up."

"Such a gentleman," she muttered, but smiled over her shoulder at him. He listened from the front as she gathered her things, closed her laptop, and then joined him back in the main lobby several minutes later.

She was sliding her arms into her coat, pulling her short, dark hair out of the collar when she looked up at him, her eyes suddenly sad. Without hesitating, he held his arms open, and she stepped forward. Sliding her arms beneath the folds of his leather jacket, she wrapped her arms around his waist and buried her face in his chest. He felt her shoulders and back expand with the deep breath she dragged in. His hands strummed through her shoulder length hair, his arms wrapped tightly around her. He didn't loosen his hold until he felt her sigh, some of the tension leaving her body.

"Better?" he asked as she stepped back. She had told him once, after her dad had passed, that hugs were most beneficial if held for longer than sixty seconds. Now, whenever she hugged him, he made sure to not let go until she was ready, no matter how long it lasted. She nodded. "Okay. Let's go, Man Hater."

She laughed, shaking her head as they exited the shop after turning off all the lights. She locked the door behind them, and they shuffled back down the sidewalk, past *Beau's*, to a solid wood door hidden in an alcove in the brick siding.

He unlocked it quickly and then held the door open, letting her in before him. They climbed the steep, creaky staircase that took them above *Beau's* below. They split at the top of the stairs, her going right, himself to the left to identical heavy wooden doors. He glanced at his watch. "Do you need extra time since you were late getting out of work?" he asked.

"No, I can be ready in an hour," she said, her hand on the doorknob of her apartment. "You really don't have to take me out tonight, Beau."

He raised his brows in annoyance, and she rolled her eyes again. "I'll see you in an hour," he said gruffly, before she disappeared into her apartment.

He showered quickly, then dressed in a pair of dark wash jeans and a black button-down shirt that he left untucked. He left the first several buttons at his throat unbuttoned, then rolled the sleeves up his forearms. The cleanest pair of black boots he owned came next, then his leather jacket again.

The dozen blush pink, peach, and yellow roses wrapped in greenery, and a small box of chocolate covered strawberries had been delivered upstairs in secret by Willow, and he picked them up as he headed out his door. He'd called in a favor to his buddy Grant Price, who owned one of the city's top-tier restaurants that overlooked the bay. He'd been able to snag a last-minute table in exchange for free coffee for the next year. Grant was also unapologetically curious about this date.

At seven o'clock he knocked on her door and he heard her call through it "Just a second!" then the door swung open, and he forgot how to breathe.

Well fuck me, he thought absently as his eyes traveled over her. The dress was simple, but dramatic. Black. A corset style bodice that cinched her waist and pushed her small breasts up. Thick straps that were tied into sweet bows at the top of each shoulder, the long ribbons hanging down her arms, fluttering with each move she made. The skirt was knee length and made entirely of layers upon layers of some kind of soft tulle like fabric, floating around her knees.

She turned away from him, and he became partially aware that she was speaking to him, but his brain was officially malfunctioning and couldn't process a single syllable. She had twisted her short hair up into some kind of sleek knot at the back of her head, a large black bow secured above the knot. Loose tendrils framed her face, and *Christ...* he nearly groaned out loud when his eyes roved over her face. Her lips had been painted a deep red. The rest of her makeup was subtle, but her eyelashes were thick and long as they framed her hazel eyes.

She picked up a pair of red stiletto heels from the entryway table and turned back toward him. She bent forward slightly, one hand bracing herself on the edge of the table as she slid the heel on the first foot, then repeated it with the other. The way she was bent forward... he was afforded a generous view of her cleavage. Something he'd never noticed before now.

Or at least, hadn't *let* himself notice, before now.

She straightened, giving him a nervous smile, wrinkling her nose as she did a slow twirl. "Well? What do you think? Knock his socks off material?"

"Yeah," he answered gruffly, then cleared his throat. "Definitely knock his socks off."

He just wasn't sure if he was talking about Ryan-The-Idiot... or himself.

Because she was *stunning*. And he was in so much fucking trouble.

CHAPTER 5

B eau was standing in her open doorway, staring at her with dark, intense eyes that made her nervous. *Maybe the dress is too much?* she worried, smoothing her hands over the soft material of her skirt.

He looked darkly handsome in his starched, dark wash jeans, and the black button-down shirt he wore beneath his leather jacket was crisp, though she could see several inches of exposed chest at the V created there by the buttons left open. His thick, dark beard had been trimmed and his dark hair that was streaked with silver shone in the light of her entryway.

Her eyes dropped to his hands and she smiled, wrinkling her nose again. He stepped forward, holding out the artful bouquet of roses that she'd watched Noelle assemble earlier that day. In his other hand, a box of their hand dipped chocolate strawberries.

"What kind of Valentine's date would I be if I didn't show up to your door with a dozen roses and a box of chocolates?" he asked, his deep voice teasing. She took them both and turned, walking into the main room of the studio apartment. She set them in the center of the small island countertop, and then turned to place the chocolate covered strawberries in the refrigerator to keep. She heard him say from behind her, "You do have something for your arms, right? You'll freeze if you go out without a jacket."

"Of course," she laughed. She picked up a black, soft wool shawl that draped over each shoulder and down her sides. A black sash tied it in the middle, keeping it closed across her body. She picked up a deep red, velvet clutch purse and glanced back at the bouquet of flowers. "You know, you didn't have to get me anything, Beau," she chastised lightly. "I know this isn't a real Valentine's date."

He winked and extended a large, work roughened hand out to her and she stepped forward, placing her hand in his. Sparks zinged up her arm at the contact, but she didn't pull away.

Beau led her back out the door and escorted her cautiously down the stairs, and she laughed when she heard him muttering about "Damn deathtraps strapped to your feet" and then "Might as well carry you so you don't slip and break an ankle" as he walked them to his car. It was a sleek, fully restored 1969 Dodge Charger. His pride and joy.

"I didn't even ask where we're going tonight. Am I horribly overdressed?" she asked, her voice coming out high pitched with panic as he slid in behind the wheel after assisting her into the passenger seat and closing the door. The engine roared to life, settling into a steady rumble as it idled. He reached out and clasped one hand over her left knee, which was bouncing with anxiety.

"You're perfect," he murmured huskily, his fingers squeezing gently. "We have a table at *The Wine Garden*."

Val gasped, turning her head sharply to look at him in the darkness of the car. Dash lights were the only thing that illuminated his face, just the slightest. "How on earth did you get a table there? On Valentine's Day of all nights?"

"Called in a favor," he said simply with a shrug, his left hand resting loosely on the steering wheel, his right hand on the shifter between them.

"You... called in a favor..." she breathed. "For a fake date. Beau..."

He turned to look at her, his dark, chocolate brown eyes meeting hers. "I'm going to need you to stop referring to tonight as a fake date. It's giving me a complex."

His tone was teasing, light, but there was something in his dark gaze that made her shiver. He'd always been an enigma, more mystery than anything else, and tonight was no different. But the way he kept looking at her... as if he were seeing her, fully, for the first time... it made butterflies take flight in her belly every time his fingers moved on the gear shift, every time his eyes met hers, the way he kept staring at her mouth. If this was a fake date, he was certainly selling it like it was real.

She almost believed it.

He pulled in and put the car in park before turning off the ignition, said a gruff, "Don't touch that door," and then he climbed out of the car. Rounding the hood, he came around and opened her door, reaching his hand down to assist her out. She shook her head at him bemusedly as she stood, but then his large, rough hand settled at the small of her back. She could feel his touch, even through the warmth of her shawl and the dress, and it made her stumble slightly.

"If you think I won't carry you across the icy sidewalk, try me," he growled close to her ear as his arm shot around her waist to steady her. Which, of course, had the exact opposite effect. Her body was pressed so close to his along her side. He smelled heavenly, his cologne a heady mix of cedar and citrus. "Only women wear toothpicks strapped to their feet in the winter."

She laughed then, glancing up at him as he maneuvered them toward the large, heavy wooden doors at the front of the restaurant. The old-fashioned, wrought iron light posts that lined the downtown's gaslight district were all lit. Wrought iron outdoor sconces were lit on either side of the doors as they entered, the warmth of the entryway a vast contrast to the cold from outside. Beau stepped forward toward the host stand, where a smartly dressed woman in a sleek black dress stood.

"Good evening, and Happy Valentine's Day. Do you have a reservation with us this evening?" the woman asked, her gaze flicking from Beau to Val, a polite smile on her face.

"Collins," Beau said, his voice low. "Grant will want to know we've arrived, as well."

"Very good, Mr. Collins, Mrs. Collins," the woman said and picked up two heavy, leather-bound menus. Val's face flamed scarlet, but the woman didn't notice as she turned away. "Follow me. Mr. Price reserved his best table for you."

They were escorted through the busy restaurant. It was small, intimate, and dimly lit, with soft instrumental music playing overhead. Each table was set with a starched white linen, a small centerpiece of red roses, and several candles were lit on each table. The hostess took them to a small table that was situated near a stone fireplace that had a blazing fire in the hearth.

Val loosened the sash around her waist and shrugged the shawl off, and the hostess took it from her, along with Beau's leather jacket. He held her chair for her, which made her smile. He really was going all out.

When they were both seated, a waiter wearing black slacks and a starched white button-down shirt stepped to the side of their table, a long, black apron tied around his waist. He set down two crystal water glasses in front of them and introduced himself. Val had stopped paying attention to the waiter, her eyes fixated on the way Beau's shoulders moved under the fabric of his black shirt, or the way the muscles in his forearms bunched when he reached for the wine list the waiter extended to him.

"Mrs. Collins? What would you like? Wine? Champagne?" Beau asked, raising his dark brown eyes to hers, a hint of a smirk tilting up one corner of his mouth. He was teasing her.

She pressed her lips together tightly to keep from giggling and blushed furiously again, dropping her gaze from his. They were seated kitty corner to one another at the small square table, instead of seated across from each other. His forearm rested on the edge of the table, dangerously close to her as she unrolled her silverware and draped the burgundy linen napkin in her lap.

"Water will be fine, to start. At least until I decide what I'm getting to eat," she said with a smile at the waiter. She had half listened as he told them the evening's special, but she would need a moment to gather herself. *Has Beau always been* this *handsome?* she thought weakly, staring at him again. Not only handsome, but... attractive, in a way that made her belly do flip flops, and lower...

Beau chuckled, and the low, husky sound of it did something to her. "I'll start with a bourbon, neat, please. And the crostini with balsamic strawberries and ricotta, as a starter. Thank you."

Val dropped her eyes to the menu in front of her, her breathing slightly erratic. Her heart was thundering in her chest. What had changed in the last hour? Wasn't he still the same old Beau, the same Beau she had known since she was barely out of pre-school?

As the waiter retreated, Beau leaned close and gestured to the menu as he said, "Whatever you want, it's yours, Val."

Her breath stalled in her throat as she stared at his mouth, which was less than a foot away from hers, where he'd leaned closer to speak to her. His dark beard was thick and looked incredibly soft. She raised her eyes to his and felt her mouth fall open at the intense way he was watching her. She knew he was referring to the menu, he *had* to be referring to the menu. Telling her to choose whatever she wanted *to eat*...

Val lowered her eyes to his mouth again, licking her lips, as she whispered huskily, "Anything I want?"

CHAPTER 6

"Anything I want?" she whispered, and the sound wound around his middle and straight to his dick.

Fuck.

Sometime in the last hour Valentina Compton had ceased to be the daughter of his parent's friends. The daughter of the man that had entrusted him to watch over his girls after his death. The pain in the ass kid that had trailed after him as a young teenager. The girl that had always been more like a little sister to him than a friend.

No, sometime in the last hour Val had become the single most intoxicating woman he'd ever met. She was stunning in that black dress, her hair pinned up, the red lipstick. Sometime in the last hour, she had become the sexiest thing he'd ever seen.

The way that she was staring at his mouth now, *fucking hell* it was taking all of his very impressive willpower not to close the distance between them and crash his mouth onto hers. Her red painted lips looked velvety soft, and he was dying to know if they felt as soft as they looked. A vision of those lips closed around his dick, the red lipstick leaving stains as she—

He reached out and tapped the menu with his index finger,

35

his elbow grazing the inside of her arm, dangerously close to the curve of her breast, and he nearly blacked out before rasping, "Whatever you want, Val. Off the menu. Nothing is off the table."

Fuck. That didn't make it any better. Now all he could think about was shoving everything off the table and spreading her out on top of it, making a meal of her while those thick thighs squeezed around his shoulders—

She lowered her eyes, her lips still parted slightly, and he watched as her hand shook as she reached for her water glass. The ice clinked lightly as she brought it to her lips. A flushed rosiness had stained her cheeks, though he rather hoped it was from the heat of the fireplace they were seated next to instead of any sort of reaction to his unintentionally provocative words.

He shifted back into his seat, leaning away from her. The scent of her perfume on her skin was making his head spin. He wanted to bury his face in her neck, inhale her deeply, taste her skin, feel the frantic fluttering of her heart at the base of her throat on his tongue...

"I think the filet mignon with the lobster tail sounds delicious," she finally said, letting her eyes drift down the menu. Raising her eyes to his, she murmured, "If that's alright?"

Glaring at her balefully, he muttered, "I already told you; whatever you want, Val. If you want three of everything, it's yours."

"Well in that case," she teased, sitting up straighter in her seat and smirking over at him. His cock twitched behind the fly of his jeans at the sight of her mouth quirking into that grin. He hated himself for it, but he wanted to watch those lips wrap around his cock. He shifted in his seat, painfully aware of how hard he was.

When the waiter returned, he gestured to Val to order, and she said softly, "I would like the filet and lobster tail, please. Medium-rare on the filet, and whatever it comes with for sides is perfect. I'd also love a glass of pinot noir, please."

He requested the bleu cheese encrusted porterhouse, along

with a side of balsamic drizzled brussels sprouts and the duchess potatoes. As the waiter stepped away, Val smiled over at him, reaching out her hand to squeeze his where it rested on the top of the table. "Thank you, Beau. For this. For tonight."

Beau raised his eyes from their hands, clasped lightly on the starched white linen, to hers. His heart was thudding painfully in his chest, and he wondered briefly if she could feel it in his wrist where hers rested on top.

A tall, barrel-chested man with dark hair and a thick beard stepped over to their table before he could respond, drawing Val's gaze from his. He raised his eyes as well, smiling when he recognized the bear of a man that had stepped toward them. He stood, pushing his chair out, at the same time extending his hand toward the man.

"Grant," Beau said, and they shook hands. "Thank you for the table." He motioned to Val. "Val, this is Grant Price, owner of *The Wine Garden*. Grant, this is Valentina Compton."

Grant extended his hand toward Val, who placed her much smaller hand in his large one. Grant shook it gently, his dark eyes twinkling as he glanced between the two. Beau's jaw tightened at the glowing appreciation on his friend's face as he stared down at Val. *Yeah, buddy, she's fucking gorgeous. Keep your damn eyeballs in your skull.* "Val, it is our pleasure to have you and Beau here this evening. I hope everything is to your liking so far?"

"Everything is wonderful," Val murmured softly, dropping her hands back into her lap when Grant released it. Beau shoved his hands into the front pockets of his jeans to keep himself from reaching out and holding Val's hand, just to replace the feel of Grant's against her skin. "Thank you so much for letting us sneak in, especially on such a busy night for you."

Grant slapped Beau on the back and the two chuckled. "What are friends for? Please, enjoy your evening."

Beau sank back into his seat as Grant walked away, stopping to greet another couple at a nearby table. The waiter showed up a moment later with Val's wine and their appetizer, setting the delicious smelling crostini between them.

The waiter withdrew and Beau reached out to serve Val one of the strawberry topped crostini, but instead of leaning back into his chair, he leaned closer. She smelled so good it made his dick twitch behind the fly of his jeans again.

"Every single man in this restaurant has had their eyes on you since we walked in that door, Val," he whispered low, his voice coming out nearly a growl. Her mouth dropped open as she raised her eyes to his. Fuck was she gorgeous. "And I guarantee every single one of them is wishing they were the one sitting here with you. Tonight, you're *my* Valentine."

CHAPTER 7

H *oly shit.*

Val could feel the rush of her breathing between her still parted lips. Beau finally leaned back in his seat, giving her much needed space, but their eyes remained locked on each other's. *He really is just so handsome,* she thought dazedly. *Unfairly, ungodly handsome.*

Taking a sip of her wine, she felt a blush stain her cheeks and her hand trembled.

In an effort to distract herself from the panty-melting hotness of the man seated beside her, she set her wine down and asked, teasing, "So, just how many of those hot chocolates did you have to suffer through making today?"

Beau laughed, leaning back in his seat. He rested one arm on the table, his fingers clasped around the crystal glass of bourbon. He raised his eyebrows and grinned as he said, "About a hundred too many, I'll be glad to not see another heart shaped sprinkle for a year."

"But they make people so happy," Val teased. They polished off the crostini and the waiter swept past, removing their empty plates as she folded her napkin back into her lap.

He shook his head with another chuckle. "That's the only reason we still serve it, one day a year." He raised his bourbon, and she watched as his mouth met the lip of the glass before his throat worked as he swallowed. "Buncha lovesick fools."

Val eyed him shrewdly, a smirk pulling up one corner of her mouth. "You can't fool me, Beau Collins. I know you're just a big softy at heart, even if you don't like to show it."

"There isn't much on me that's soft, Val," he murmured low, his eyes dropping to her lips. Holy fuck. Heat rushed over her chest and up her neck. And lower.

The moment was interrupted by the waiter as he stopped at their table. Val dropped her eyes to her lap, taking a shuddering breath in. Was it the wine that was making her overheated? Or was it Beau?

She glanced up at him as the waiter placed their plates in front of each of them, and she bit her lower lip. Definitely Beau.

Beau ordered another bourbon, though Val declined a second glass of wine, still nursing the first one. The food in front of them looked divine and smelled delicious. Her mouth watered as she picked up her silverware.

Acutely aware of Beau's presence at her side, she cut daintily into the filet and speared it with her fork before bringing it to her lips. Her eyelids fluttered closed at the first taste. His dark, low chuckle snapped her eyes open and she rolled her eyes at him when he grinned at her.

"Oh my god," she moaned after the second bite. "This is... incredible."

"I'll make sure to tell Van you said that," he chuckled again, slicing into his porterhouse.

"Van?" she asked after swallowing a bite of lobster.

"Sulivan Laurance; he's always gone by Van. He's Grant's partner and the chef here," Beau said, nodding his head toward the back of the room where the kitchen doors were located. "Actually, I'd be surprised if he doesn't make an appearance

42

tonight. They were both ravenously curious about my date tonight."

"Oh? His partner?" she breathed, her fork stopping at her mouth.

Beau chuckled and rested his elbow on the table as he leaned closer to her. "*Business* partner, Val."

The blush that stained her cheeks burned all the way to her toes. "Oh. Are they friends of yours?"

"I went to school with Grant, we've known each other for a long time. He met Van about five years ago through a mutual friend. Van was new to the area and wanted to open a restaurant, and Grant needed something to keep himself occupied after... well, he needed a project. Something to start fresh. So they opened *The Wine Garden* together."

Val nodded. She understood the necessity of needing to start fresh. She took a drink of her wine and sighed.

"Starting over isn't a bad thing, you know."

She snapped her eyes to his. *How does he do that?* she wondered dazedly. How this man can so easily read her mind...

"I know," she whispered, nodding just the slightest. "I just... I'm not..." she closed her eyes and set her fork down, before opening them again. "Starting over hasn't been a bad thing. It's just... sad. Like I failed. I'm thirty-two and had to move back home because my marriage fell apart, and I couldn't save it. And now I'm alone and after the last few months of attempting to date again... it just feels so hopeless. The thought of continuing to go on awful first dates is exhausting. Who is going to want someone like me?" She waved her hand and rolled her eyes then in a self-deprecating way when Beau opened his mouth to respond. "Sorry. That's not what I meant to say. I already decided I'm done dating. I just have to get to the point that I'm okay with the idea of being alone again. For however long."

"Did you want to save your marriage, Val?" Beau asked, lowering his own fork to his plate.

"No," she whispered, shaking her head as she stared at him. "But I still struggle with this overwhelming feeling of failure. If I'd been better, done more—"

Beau's hand snapped out and she gasped when his fingers gripped her chin in his fingers, holding her still as he leaned forward.

"If I ever hear you talk about yourself like that again, Valentina, I will put you over my knee and turn that pretty ass pink. I don't care how old you are or the fact that I used to babysit you." Her teeth sank into her lower lip. His eyes followed the movement before they slid back up to hers, and his dark eyes were intense as he stared at her. "Wes was a douchebag and didn't deserve one tenth of what you gave to him, and the saying 'the trash takes itself out' has never been truer when it comes to that cheating asshole. Ryan is an idiot for letting you walk away. Those moron's that had the fortune to go on a date with you and not enough sense in their brains to know what they had for even the briefest of moments… well, that's their loss. Any man would be lucky to have any part of you, Val. Do you understand me?"

She nodded, only as much as his fingers still gripping her chin would allow. "Yes," she breathed on a whisper.

He nodded once, then stroked her jaw with the pad of his thumb as his eyes dropped back to her mouth. She held her breath. *He wouldn't… would he?*

But then he released his hold on her chin and leaned back into his chair, and Val thought her heart was going to pound its way out of her chest. Could he see it hammering away above the neckline of her dress?

God, she hoped not.

CHAPTER 8

*D*on't kiss her.
Don't. Fucking. Kiss her.
Fuck.

Beau forced himself to lean back into his chair and away from her. Away from that too tempting mouth. Forced himself to pick up his fork and take a stab at the duchess potatoes on his plate. Forced his hand to rise and take the bite of potatoes off his fork between his teeth.

She shifted in her seat beside him. Her breathing was shallow, ragged, her chest rising and falling with each panting breath. Those red painted lips closed around another bite of her food, and he forced the groan that rumbled up his chest to remain silent. His cock was hard as steel in his pants.

Guilt made his chest ache, and he fought the urge to press his hand over his sternum. He wasn't supposed to be thinking about Val like this. He wasn't supposed to have a raging hard-on for her. It was Val, the girl he'd known for three decades. The girl he'd chased around the yard with grasshoppers as she screamed in pretend terror. The girl he'd given rides home from school to. The girl he'd promised her father he would look out for.

But fuck if he couldn't stop from thinking about her, making his dick even harder. He was sure he had to be leaking precum at this point. He was so hard it hurt. Shifting in his own seat, he attempted to reposition his aching cock in his pants, but the shift just made it worse.

Unsorted inventory. Spilled coffee grounds in my sock. Curdled milk in the walk in. Fuck, he'd think of *anything*, to make this hard-on go away!

He glanced up when someone stopped beside their table, and he made his best attempt at a smile, though he was sure it came out more as a grimace. There was also no way he was going to be able to stand up and shake the man's hand; if he did, the raging erection he was sporting was going to be on full display, right in front of and level with Val's face.

So, he remained seated, though he did set his knife and fork down to reach out for the hand being extended to him as his friend spoke. "Good evening. I do hope everything has been to your liking. Beau, thank you for bringing such a beautiful woman into our restaurant."

Beau nodded, but his teeth clenched together so tightly his jaw ached when he watched Val's cheeks tinge pink again with a blush as she stared up at the stupidly handsome chef. He extended his hand to Val, who placed hers in his, and they shook briefly. A pristine white chef jacket was buttoned closed, and once the handshake was done, the man placed his hands behind his back.

"Van, this is Val, a good friend of mine. Val, this is Van, the executive chef, and Grant's business partner." He forced his tone to remain neutral through the introductions. Though he knew Van would never overstep, he also didn't like the way he was staring at her. She was his.

"Grant came back and told me you'd arrived, and with a beauty on your arm. I had to come see for myself; and must I say, he was not exaggerating."

Val made a sound that came out like a choked sort of giggle, and Beau narrowed his eyes on his buddy. "Alright, Casanova. Don't you have a kitchen to terrorize?"

Van laughed, tipping back his blonde head, but then he winked down at Val. "I'll leave you two to your meals. Val, it was wonderful to meet you. You make this old man look good." Beau rolled his eyes and smirked over at Val, who blushed again. "Beau, you grumpy old cuss, make sure you bring her back to see us again soon."

Beau nodded and raised the glass of bourbon to his lips to take a sip before clearing his throat. "You're a menace, Van."

Van chuckled as he walked away, back toward the heavy doors that led into the commercial kitchen. Val laughed and shook her head as she took a drink of her wine, and she glanced over at him over the rim of her wine glass. He swallowed hard when their eyes met and held.

"Sorry about that," he said gruffly, notching his chin toward the door that Van had disappeared into. The waiter took their empty plates, and Beau placed his napkin on the table in front of him.

"Self-proclaimed bachelor Beau Collins is on a Valentine's date," she said softly, leaning toward him, her eyes shining with mischief. "That's got to be something newsworthy around this town. You might have to start fighting off Mama's that are looking to marry off their daughters."

He couldn't control the shiver of aversion that shook him, and the laugh that erupted out of Val made him grin. He liked seeing her happy. She didn't smile enough anymore. He'd missed it.

Shit, he'd missed *her*.

The waiter returned to their table with a puffy chocolate raspberry souffle dusted with confectioners' sugar into the shape of a heart, a sprig of mint and a fresh raspberry perched on top. The waiter set it down between them and Beau raised his eyes in question. "Compliments of Chef Laurance."

49

Val oooh'd over the dessert. Beau chuckled lightly and handed her one of the spoons perched on the side of the plate. "I think we're supposed to share this. You don't have cooties, do you?"

"Of course not, but all boys have cooties," Val laughed again, throwing him a teasing glance. She took the spoon from him and waved it idly and winked at him. "I'm pretty sure I'm up to date on my cootie shots, so I think I'm safe from you."

Beau laughed out loud, a full grin pulling across his face. He reached out and tugged lightly on one of the tendrils of hair that framed her face. "You're always safe with me."

CHAPTER 9

They battled with their spoons over the last bite of souffle, but Beau graciously let her win. After a second glass of wine, Val was just tipsy enough and deliciously full of the divine food to be nearly boneless.

"I know we should get up and let them turn over this table, but I don't want to move," she murmured wistfully. "I don't know that I *can* move. That was all… incredible. I can't believe I've never been here."

Well, that wasn't entirely true. She knew why she'd never been into this restaurant before now. It was intimate, romantic. And nothing about her life in the last year had been either intimate *or* romantic.

Beau chuckled again, and the low, husky rumble of it made goosebumps flash across her skin. The butterflies that had remained present in her midriff since she'd open the door to him at her apartment fluttered around crazily in her middle. He stood, then reached one of those strong, capable looking hands toward her. "Come on, I'll roll you out of here."

Val's mouth dropped open in a surprised laugh but placed her hand in his. The warmth of it as he closed his fingers around hers made those butterflies do nosedives in her stomach, sending heat to the very core of her. God, it had been a long time since she'd felt arousal like this...

But it was Beau. Beau, the man that had always watched out for her. That would never see her as anything other than the add-on sister he'd never had. The man that had made a promise to her dying father to take care of her, her mother, and her sisters. The man that would willingly take a pathetic, lonely woman out on a fake Valentine's date. That's all this was.

And she needed to remind her traitorous, sex-starved body of that fact before it got any crazy ideas. Any *crazier* ideas.

Because lord was her brain in overdrive.

Rising to her feet with Beau's hand still clasped around hers, she smoothed the tulle of her skirt down over her hips with her free hand. She picked up the red velvet clutch and together—hands *still* clasped—they walked toward the front of the restaurant. She hoped that Beau couldn't feel her hand tremble in his.

As they approached the hostess stand, the hostess disappeared and returned with Beau's leather jacket and her wool shawl. Taking the shawl from the hostess, Beau finally released her hand and held the shawl up for her to slide her arms into. She reached for the long ties on either side of her waist, but he brushed her hands aside and she thought she just might die when he began to secure them into a bow at her waist. Cinching her up, he ran his fingers up the overlapping sides as they crossed over her chest, tugging lightly until it was closed clear up to her chin.

Val's heart thudded in her chest as she stared up at him. She knew her mouth was hanging open dumbly, but her brain wouldn't communicate with the rest of her to shut the damn thing. His fingers strummed along the column of her throat, and she sucked in a staggered breath.

Then, as calmly as he'd tucked her into her shawl, he backed away, turning to retrieve his jacket from the hostess and slide it on his arms. Adjusting it over his wide shoulders, she simply stood in front of him, completely dumbstruck. Was she that buzzed, or was Beau really just that intoxicating all on his own?

Beau's hand at the small of her back as he led her out the door was warm and steady. His hand slid around her waist as they made their way down the brick-paved walkway to the sidewalk, dusted with snow and slick with ice. He reached out and opened the passenger door for her, assisting her into the low riding vehicle before closing the door and hurrying around the hood. He slid in behind the wheel and started it, adjusting the thermostat and the blowers to start warming up the interior of the car. Val shivered and pressed her frozen fingers under the outside of her thighs so that she was sitting on them.

Teeth chattering, she turned to look at him as he rubbed his hands together to warm them. He chuckled through the dim interior, one of the cities wrought iron light posts shining flickering beams of light into the car. "It should warm up in just a few. I don't have remote start."

"I wouldn't expect a vintage car to have remote start, Beau," she laughed, teeth still chattering, but the interior was already warming up, helping her muscles to relax just a little. He reached out and adjusted the direction of the blower so that it was focused more on her, and she sighed when the heat really started to sink into her bones. She untucked her hands from under her thighs and reached back for the seat belt, pulling it across her to snap it into place. Val watched under her lashes as Beau did the same, and then he was shifting gears and pulling out of the parking spot and into the narrow two-lane street. The wind howled outside of the car, but it was toasty inside.

The drive back to their apartment building was short and quiet, neither of them breaking the silence other than the soft rock music playing from the car's stereo. Beau pulled into his designated parking spot outside of their apartments and turned toward her. "Stay put."

She nodded and her lips pulled into a grin as he climbed out of the car and rounded the hood again, coming to open her door. Assisting her out of the low seat, his hand was once again wrapped around hers firmly.

"I promise I won't fall, Beau," she said with a roll of her eyes when he refused to release her hand as they walked the short way to the door.

"And my mother would skin me alive if I didn't escort a woman wearing deathtraps on her feet on an icy sidewalk," Beau muttered darkly, but she could see the dimple in his cheek peeking as he tried to suppress a smirk. He squeezed her hand. "I won't hesitate to carry you, so don't tempt me."

"Such a gentleman," she sighed as he held the door open to their building. And still, he refused to release her, even as they started their way up the long flight of stairs that led to the landing that separated their two apartments at the top. He stepped with her toward her door, and she squeezed his hand gently as she murmured quietly, "Thank you for dinner, Beau."

He finally released her hand so she could dig into the velvet clutch in her other hand for her key.

"Do you want to come in?" she asked as she stepped inside, holding the door open for him to follow her. "You have to help me eat the strawberries you brought. I can't possibly eat them all myself."

She held her breath, watching him as he tried to come up with an excuse not to, but then he sighed and stepped through the door and let her close it behind him. She untied the sash at her waist, drawing the shawl off her shoulders and hanging it on a hook by the door before she led the way into the main room. Her heels tapped lightly on the hardwood floor as she crossed to the refrigerator, pulling it open and producing a chilled bottle of champagne and the chocolate covered strawberries she'd placed in there earlier.

She handed the bottle to him wordlessly as he reached the tiny island in the center of the kitchen, where the bouquet of roses sat in the center. She set the box of strawberries down and crossed to a floating shelf along the wall and plucked two stemmed champagne flutes down before returning to the island. She then crossed the room again, queuing up a small, portable Bluetooth speaker by the kitchen sink. Val scrolled through her phone and picked a Spotify playlist of classic slow rock love ballads, just because of the occasion.

She walked around the rooms and lit two candles in the living room and one in the kitchen, turning the rest of the lights down low.

He'd managed to get the decorative foil off the champagne, then wrapped the neck with a dishtowel and removed the cork with a sharp pop. He poured the effervescent alcohol into first one flute, then the other, handing her one.

She raised her glass toward him, and she watched as he clinked his to hers gently, the light tinkling of the crystal the only sound in the room other than the quiet music that drifted over to them.

"May crappy, cheating ex-husbands and douchebag dates be a thing of the past," she murmured softly, raising the glass to her lips. "And may we both be happy in our singlehood."

Beau shook his head, laughing quietly. "That's a terrible toast. You can't make that a Valentine's Day toast."

"Oh yeah? Well, what *should* I toast to?" she asked, her tone snarky. "That tall, tattooed, bearded lumberjack that's going to give me two dozen orgasms?"

"I'm going to give you a small piece of advice, Val," he murmured low, leaning his back against the edge of the island, turning his head to look at her with those intense dark eyes. "You can't be afraid to start over again. You don't need a new chapter, sweetheart. Start a whole new book."

Tears stung her nose and sprang to her eyes and she blinked rapidly so he wouldn't see. She took a long sip of her champagne, and watched out of the corner of her eyes as he lifted his glass to his lips. He made a face as the bubbly liquid met his tongue, and she laughed lightly. "I have some whiskey if you'd like to sip that instead?"

"No, this is fine. It's just been a long time since I've had any reason to drink champagne," he chuckled, setting the glass down on the counter beside them.

"Would you like to sit?" she asked, pointing to the couch across the room. He nodded, then picked up his glass again and followed her to the tiny living room. She set the box of strawberries she'd grabbed on the coffee table along with her glass as he lowered his frame onto one side of the couch.

"These heels have to go," she groaned, kicking them off with a sigh, her poor feet aching from the high arch of the heel. She sank down flat footed and laughed in relief as she stretched her arches out before sinking down into the opposite corner of the couch. "They're beautiful, but sometimes I don't think they're worth the pain."

He patted his lap and she raised her eyes to his. He gave her a hard look and patted his lap again. "Come on, I don't bite. I'll massage your feet."

"You're really committed to this fake date," she laughed dryly, shaking her head, but when he patted his thigh again, she sighed. Val was incredibly happy that she'd taken the time to give herself a quick pedicure while she was getting ready earlier.

She shifted, leaning her back against the armrest of the couch and carefully raised her feet into his lap, cautious not to let the layers of her skirt ride up too far. He grunted in answer and picked up one of her feet, cradling it in both of his large, warm hands. At the first run of his thumb from the ball of her foot, down the aching arch, to her heel, she gasped sharply, and an involuntary moan escaped her. She clamped her hand over her mouth in horror and stared at him with wide eyes. He just chuckled and did it again. Her eyes fluttered closed in ecstasy.

She cradled her champagne glass between her hands in her

lap, too distracted to drink it as he methodically soothed her aching feet. He paid attention to her toes, her heels, the arches, and even went as far as to massage the muscles of her calves. She was nearly delirious when he finally stopped after squeezing each foot one last time.

"That... was even better than twelve orgasms," she sighed, letting her head fall back to stare at the ceiling. She brought her head back down to look at him. His dark features were shadowed in the low light, the candlelight flickering along the walls and the ceiling. She raised her arms over her head, first untying the ribbon and setting it aside on the coffee table, before releasing her hair from the pins that held the twist in place. Her hair fell around her shoulders in waves and she sighed when the pressure of the pins against her head finally abated. Val pulled her feet from his lap and shifted, leaning over to the box of chocolate covered strawberries and plucking one out of its wrapping. They were ready for consumption without having to maneuver around the stems. She bit down on it and chewed, then chased it with a swallow of her champagne and she nodded in bliss. "Best combination ever."

"I'll take your word for it," he murmured, taking a swallow of his own champagne.

"Mmmm," she hummed, leaning over to pick up another one. She shifted again, rising up on her knees as she moved closer to him, one arm balancing herself on the back of the couch, as she extended her hand toward his mouth. "Try."

He shook his head, just once, staring at the fruit between her fingers before raising those impossibly dark eyes to her own.

"Please?" she whispered, inching her hand closer. "They're too good not to share."

She held her breath as he stared at her for what felt like a lifetime before he slowly leaned forward. His lips parted and she settled the chocolate dipped fruit between them, his straight, white teeth sinking into the soft flesh of the strawberry, near her

DANIELLE BAKER

fingers. His lips and beard grazed her fingertips and she gasped silently. His eyes never left hers as he chewed and then swallowed. She raised the small, remaining bite of the strawberry toward him once more, and he closed his lips around her fingers, fully this time. His tongue laved the pad of her thumb, his beard tickling her fingers, and she thought she just might die from the eroticism of it.

She swallowed hard, still staring at him, and she realized her breathing was erratic and her heart was hammering in her chest as he released her fingers. He swallowed the bite of strawberry and then dropped his eyes to her mouth, which was parted as she dragged in short, rapid breaths.

"I need you to tell me to go home," she heard him whisper roughly, his voice husky and dark. It skittered over her. He remained impossibly still beside her. "Tell me good night, and tell me not to do this, Val."

"And what if I don't?" she asked, her voice shaking just the slightest. She dropped her eyes to his mouth, shifting just a tiny bit closer to him. The arm that was resting on the back of the couch behind him was very nearly touching his hard shoulders. She moved, slowly, bringing her hand to the back of his head, ruffling into the strands of dark hair at his nape. It was as soft to touch as it looked. She felt his breath hitch in his throat at the contact.

Bravely, she lowered her other hand to his bewhiskered jaw and cupped it in her palm, letting her nails scratch lightly against his beard. Then she slid her palm down the side of his neck as she shifted again, moving closer to him. His own breathing had become ragged as she touched him, moved nearer to him, but his eyes remained steadily on hers.

"*Val*," he growled low. A warning.

Or a plea.

60

CHAPTER 10

She leaned forward and pressed her mouth to his.

When he didn't react for several long heartbeats, she felt mortification well up inside her chest and she pulled away quickly, dropping her gaze to the buttons on his shirt. "Oh God, I'm sorry—"

Hands bracketed her face and pulled her back to him, his mouth crashing onto hers with a low groan. She fell forward slightly, catching herself on his shoulders, her fingers tightening into fists in the fabric of his shirt as his tongue speared between her lips and sank into her mouth. His head twisted, deepening the kiss, his mouth slanting over hers voraciously. They kissed until they were both breathless, tongues tangling. His beard abraded her deliciously. Wet heat had pooled between her thighs. Desire like she hadn't felt in ages roared through her veins.

He drew his mouth from hers, pressing his forehead to hers and rolling it there, her face still clasped between his large, work roughened hands.

"Tell me to go," he groaned, his eyes clenched shut tightly, even as he continued to roll his forehead along hers. "Tell me to leave, Val."

"I can't," she gasped, her fingers tightening in his shirt. "I won't."

He kissed her again, one hand sliding behind her neck to clasp her nape, beneath her hair. He tasted like bourbon, champagne, and strawberries. His kiss deepened again, and she moaned into his mouth. She was so wet. Aching.

Sliding one leg over both of his thighs until her knees were straddling his hips on the cushions of the couch, she settled on his lap. Her dress had bunched and pooled around her thighs. Shifting forward, she gasped audibly when she felt him, hard, against the junction of her thighs.

Her gasp had him yanking away from her sharply, moving her roughly off of him and onto the couch once more. He stood, striding away from her with jerky, stilted movements. Beau stood with his back to her, where he'd left her on the couch. He blew out a ragged breath and scrubbed his hand over his face and down his jaw, before letting his chin drop down until it nearly touched his chest.

Rejection tasted bitter in her mouth, made her chest ache painfully. But then she watched as he palmed the front of his jeans as he raised his head with a low groan, and she knew he wanted this. Wanted her.

Standing on silent feet, she crossed to where he stood, sliding her palms up his hard back. He flinched slightly but didn't pull away from her.

"I need to go," he growled, his voice unsteady. His head turned just enough to allow her to see him in profile. He took several steps toward the door.

"Beau," she whispered, a soft plea. He turned toward her, and she could feel the heat in his gaze, the tension rolling off of his body. "You said whatever I want tonight."

His jaw clenched and his lips tightened, even as his dark eyes speared into her own. They were hot. Barely reined in desire sparked in them.

Reaching behind her, she lowered the zipper of her dress. She took a deep, courage bolstering breath and then shimmied, letting the dress fall to the floor at her feet with a rustled whisper. She stood before him, completely naked except for a pair of black lace panties.

She watched as his Adam's apple bobbed thickly, his white-hot gaze roving over her nakedness. The candlelight flickered wildly, casting them each in shadow and light. His hands balled into fists at his sides and his chest rose and fell rapidly with each breath he took.

She stepped out of the pool of fabric, taking two tentative steps toward him. She hadn't been naked in front of anyone in over a year. Sex hadn't seemed to be something Ryan was particularly interested in, satisfied with heavy petting after their dates. It had been so long since she'd felt a man between her legs, felt the weight of someone pressing against her, into her. It had been nearly two years since she'd had an orgasm that wasn't self-induced with her faithful vibrator.

She was acutely aware of his eyes still on her. They cataloged every inch of her skin. Her hips were wide, thighs heavier than she'd like and striped with faint stretch marks. Her stomach wasn't perfectly flat, her lower belly soft, but her ribcage was narrow. Her breasts were small but round, her nipples tipped and pointed in the slight chill of the room.

"You said whatever I wanted tonight," she repeated as she drew closer to him, slowly, as if trying not to spook him. He stared at her, his gaze intense. "Please. Beau…hold me and don't let go until I say to. Don't go."

Whatever had been holding him back snapped; she saw it in his eyes. He muttered a rough, "Fuck," and strode forward, wrapping his arms around her tightly. One hand buried itself in her hair, his other arm banded around her waist. His large, strong hand squeezed a handful of one of her ass cheeks as his mouth crashed against hers again.

This kiss was carnal, heady, and rough. A claiming. He wasn't gentle, his teeth nipping at her bottom lip until she gasped sharply. He soothed it with his tongue and then took her mouth again deeply. He pressed their bodies tightly together and she wound her arms around his waist, fisting her fingers in the fabric of the back of his shirt.

"You should have let me leave," he growled against her mouth, and she trembled slightly. She was shaking. He caught her jaw in his hands, tilting her face up to his. "Tonight, you're mine, Val. Do you understand? I'm going to make you come so hard you see stars."

She nodded against his mouth mutely, and then he clasped her beneath the curves of her bottom and lifted her. She squeaked in alarm, wrapping her arms around his shoulders and her legs around his hips as he deftly carried her through the tiny apartment toward her bedroom. He deposited her on her back on the bed and his hands dropped to the scrap of lace that was the only thing keeping her from being completely naked. He shimmied them down her thighs and tossed them aside, his eyes running over her. His fingers made quick work of the buttons down his shirt before he tossed that aside too, at the same time toeing off his boots. He stood at the foot of her bed in nothing but jeans that were tented at his fly. His chest rose and fell, his shoulders, arms, and chest heavily tattooed.

"Jesus, Val," he muttered darkly from above her and she blushed before his hands slid over her thighs, up her hips, to the curve of her waist again. "You're fucking exquisite."

She fairly glowed under his praise and reached for him at the same time that he lowered himself over her, pressing his body along hers fully as his mouth found hers once more. She slid her hands into the hair at the back of his head, rolling her hips against his until he hissed out a string of curses, dropping his mouth to the curve of her throat. His fingers plucked at one tight nipple, making her arch off the bed with a sharp cry.

He pressed kisses along her shoulder, collarbones, pressed his tongue to the frantic fluttering of her heartbeat at the base of her throat. All the while, he whispered dark, sexy words to her. "You're so fucking beautiful. Fuck, these tits," he groaned hoarsely, dropping his mouth to take one peaked nipple into his mouth. Her fingers tightened in his hair as she writhed beneath him. "I thought I'd never seen anything as beautiful as you in that dress tonight, Val. But you naked in front of me...you take my fucking breath away."

He showed each breast the same adoring attention before kissing lower, down her belly. He knelt on the floor and wrapped his arms beneath her knees, pulling her toward the edge of the bed.

"Oh!" she cried, propping herself on her elbows as his breath ghosted over the junction of her thighs. He grinned up at her, pressing his mouth hotly to the inside of her left thigh. When he came away, there was a dark bruise there and she gasped. "Beau, you don't have to—"

"This was all I could think about at dinner," he rasped, his voice low and dangerous. "All I could think about. Shoving everything off that table and making this pretty little pussy my meal instead."

"Holy shit," she moaned, dropping back and throwing one arm over her eyes as the other hand found purchase in his hair. His lips were dragging over her clit, his beard tickling her, and then his tongue lashed out and she shuddered. She tried to pull away, but he wrapped his heavily muscled, tattooed arms around her thighs where they were spread over his shoulders. His hands slid up to press, palms flat, against her abdomen. Hands spread wide in the gap between her hip bones, fingers pressing into the softness of her belly as he suckled and licked and stroked. His tongue danced around her clit, pushed inside her even as he hummed with approval as she cried out at his ministrations. One of his arms released her thigh, his hand disappearing between her thighs as his tongue returned to her clit, circling deftly. And then his lips closed around that bundle of nerves at the same time he pressed two fingers inside her as deep as he could, flicking his fingers against that magical spot deep inside.

"Oh *fuck*," she cried, circling her hips against his mouth and hand as her thighs began to shake uncontrollably around his shoulders. The hand still pressed flat against her stomach flexed, pressing down even as he continued to flick his fingers inside her, his mouth deftly suckling her clit. "Beau, I'm—"

She felt more than heard his answering hum of approval as she came hard around his fingers, against his tongue. The climax tore through her, her entire body shuddering with the intensity of it, her back arching off the bed. When it had abated, she slumped into the mattress, a panting mess.

He gave her only a moment of relief before starting again. This time it barreled through her without warning, so quickly she couldn't draw a breath. She'd never in her life come so hard and *so fast*.

She was panting, stars indeed dancing behind her eyes, when he crawled up her limp body. He kissed her thoroughly, and she blushed furiously at the taste of herself on his lips, his tongue. His beard abraded her cheeks.

"We're not done yet," he warned against her mouth. "I'm going to feel you come on my cock, Val."

"Ohmygod," she moaned, tossing her head back against the mattress. She ran her hands over his naked chest, down his sides. Was this really happening? This was Beau... and lord was he magnificent. She looked up at him, wide eyed, when her hands encountered nothing but the bare flesh of his hips. She had been so deliriously distracted by the strength of her orgasms that she hadn't noticed him take his jeans or his underwear off before he'd climbed up with her. His abdomen pressed between her spread thighs. "I haven't... haven't been with anyone since Wes."

He kissed her, slowly, thoroughly. "It's okay, Val," he whispered huskily when he released her mouth. "We don't have to do anything you don't want—"

"No, that's not..." she whispered, her face flaming. "It's just... been a long time, is all. Don't stop. Don't go."

He raised up on his knees between her spread thighs and she lowered her gaze to take in all of him. His cock was hard and long and thick, a bead of precum on the tip. She reached out her hand and wrapped her fingers around him. She watched as his eyes slid closed, his head tipping back slightly. He was big... much bigger than her ex-husband had been. Girthier, longer. As she moved her hand, he shifted his hips back and forth, drawing the steely length through her hand again and again. The muscles in his abdomen bunched and tightened beneath a layer of soft flesh and his thighs flexed. His body was thick and soft in places, but well maintained. His eyes burned into hers as he dropped one of his hands to cover hers, pumping his hips into their hands wrapped around his cock.

"Are you sure, Val?" he husked down at her. "You say the word and I'll stop."

"No," she whimpered, tightening her fingers around him just the slightest, which made his hips jerk, and a low gasp was torn from his lips. "Don't stop. Don't go. Please. I need you inside me." She licked her lips then and blushed, whispering, "I... when I decided to try dating again... there are condoms in the bathroom."

"I have one," he murmured and nodded, shifting, but he ran his fingers down the center of her chest, between her breasts as his eyes speared into hers. "But I'm glad to know you're being careful. That's a good girl."

"I'm... I'm clean. And still on birth control," she said, blushing again, even as his words washed over her. They did something to her.

"I always wear a condom, Val," he said gently, leaning down to press a chaste kiss to her mouth. "Always. I'm extremely careful, too."

He shifted to the side, picking up a foil square that she hadn't noticed him toss onto the bed earlier. He tore the packet open with his teeth and then rolled the condom on before lowering his large frame to cover her again.

She shifted her hips, drawing her knees up on either side of his hips as he kissed her. Her arms slid beneath his, her hands sliding up to cup his muscled shoulders. He had braced himself on one of his forearms, and then he was positioning himself at her entrance.

The hand that was between her thighs, where he began pressing into her so slowly, came up and wrapped around the outside of her thigh, hitching it up higher as he pressed in. She gasped at the intrusion; her body unaccustomed to being so full after so long. His mouth left her lips, and he pressed his forehead against hers, staying that way until he had buried himself all the way in. It was tight, almost painfully so, and Val shifted her hips against his. He groaned audibly, his breath fanning over her face, and he rocked his hips against hers several times, not pulling out.

The friction, the angle, everything was magic. He was magic.

And then he started to move. Slow, deep strokes that pulled him nearly all the way out before sliding back in as deep as he could go, as deep as she could take him. Over and over again. The fingers clasped around her thigh squeezed tight, pushing her leg up higher still, which made the angle of his hips driving into hers deeper, and she cried out sharply on a keening cry. She reached for his lips with her own, her hands sliding from his shoulders to his waist, where she pressed in an effort to get closer. She was coming again. Her thighs shook as her body convulsed around his where he was pressed so deep.

"That's it, sweetheart," he growled against her mouth raggedly, a smile curving his lips as she continued to spasm around him. "Oh yes. Fuck that feels so good. You come so good for me, Val."

She was a mess. Her head tossed against the bed, her fingers scrabbling at his skin. He was so warm against her, the contrast of his hardness to everything that was soft on her, the rough texture of his body hair as it abraded the inside of her thighs, her breasts, her neck and cheeks and chin where his beard scratched her deliciously. She had missed this.

He continued to whisper filthy, beautiful things into her ear, against her skin, his breathing ragged as he moved over her, inside her. Again and again. He raised up onto his knees and brought her legs up so that her ankles hung over his shoulders. He pressed a hot, open-mouthed kiss to the inside of her ankle, his fingers digging into the groove made by her thighs and hips.

His hips slammed into hers, rougher than before, the front of his hips slapping against the backs of her thighs. He reached between their bodies and his fingers found her clit, circling it deftly. She moaned long and low.

"Can you do another one?" he asked darkly from above her. She shook her head, eyes pinched tightly shut, her lower lip caught between her teeth. It was too much. "One more, sweetheart. One more. I want to feel you come again."

He continued to manipulate her clit with his fingers as he pumped into her. She was shaking, gasping for air, her entire body taut with how hard he was making her come, over and over again.

"*Beau*," she sobbed on a low cry, her abdominal muscles pulling tight as she came for a fourth time. He was trying to kill her; she was sure of it. Her chest was aching, and stars danced behind her tightly closed lids. "*Oh please—*"

"Look at me," he demanded roughly, and her eyes popped open, clashing with his. He dropped her legs as she continued to come around him, his restraint crumbling. Her legs banded around his hips as he dropped forward onto his hands on either side of her body, his hips slamming into hers hard. He fucked her through her orgasm and straight into another one, or maybe it was just the same one and it never stopped, she wasn't sure. Her body wasn't hers anymore. It belonged to him. His dark, intense eyes never left hers, and she had never felt more seen or more beautiful than she did in that moment.

His hips stuttered and he pushed into her once, twice more, before stilling, his chest heaving as he came with a guttural, savage groan, his forehead dropping to her shoulder. She felt his spasms deep inside, against the inner walls of her sex, each pulse stealing her breath.

He lowered his body down to hers before rolling them to their sides. He remained inside her, and every so often she would feel another aftershock ripple through each of them. His hands roamed over her bare back, pressing her chest against his as she rested with her head in the curve of his shoulder, his chin pressed against the top of her head.

Finally, he pulled out of her. Pressing a kiss to her forehead, he murmured, "I'll be right back," and then he rolled to the edge of the bed and stood. She blushed as he removed the used condom and then he disappeared into the bathroom. He was gone for a few minutes and then returned with a warm, damp cloth. She flushed with embarrassment as he moved onto the bed, gripping her knee and separating her legs. He was thorough and attentive, and then disappeared for just a moment before returning to bed. He gathered her into his arms, and she pressed her cheek to his chest, where she could hear his heart beating. Beau pulled the comforter up over them.

Val was listening to his breathing and the steady cadence of his heart beneath her ear when she whispered, "I don't want you to think you have to stay, Beau..."

She squeezed her eyes shut when she felt him shift, preparing for him to stand and take his leave. Instead, she felt him press a kiss to her forehead before he tipped her chin up. "You asked me to hold you until you said to let go. Are you saying you want me to let go?"

Her heart ached at the words and the unfamiliar softness in his gaze as he stared down at her. She shook her head, drawing circles on his bare chest with her fingertip. "No. I don't want you to let go. Not yet."

He leaned down and kissed her gently on the lips. "Then I'll stay until you're ready, Val."

CHAPTER 11

*fter Val's breathing had turned slow and deep, signaling that she had fallen asleep, Beau lay awake, arm wrapped around her frame, holding her to him in the dark. He could hear the wind as it whipped outside the second story window. She didn't have the thick, blackout shades covering her bedroom window that he did in his apartment across the hall, and the streetlight from across the road shined faintly through the fabric of her curtains. It cast just enough light to cast her features into relief from the shadows, and he couldn't help but watch her in the quiet of the room. Her music still played softly from the living room.

As gently as he could, he disentangled himself from her and stood, pulling his boxer briefs up his legs. Padding out the bedroom door on bare feet, he crossed the tiny apartment that mirrored his and blew out the candles she'd lit earlier, then turned off the Bluetooth speaker in the kitchen. The absence of the music cast his thoughts into deafening, violent spirals in his head.

I just fucked Valentina Compton. Felt her come on my fingers, my tongue... my dick. And I liked it. Immensely.

This… was not how he had envisioned their *fake date* ending tonight.

He was supposed to say good night to her at the door, kiss her cheek, and send her off to bed; alone. He had offered to take her out to take her mind off being dumped the night before. Granted, Ryan Kaylor was an idiot of the grandest kind, and he doubted her hurt feelings were simply more than stung pride, rather than any solid feelings for the man.

I just hate seeing her so morose, her usual vibrance so lackluster. That's all.

He snorted in the dark, leaning on the island counter with his hands gripping the edge so tightly his knuckles turned white. *Yeah, right.*

He'd been sick to his stomach with a deep sense of possessive protectiveness when he'd learned she was returning to dating. The last several months of watching her go on shitty dates with men who probably didn't know the first thing about treating a woman right were gut wrenchingly miserable. There wasn't a man in the area worthy of her. She was everything good in the world; so full of light and hope and beauty.

He'd known Ryan for years. He was well known around town, a decent guy. Recently divorced himself and a newly single father to his twelve-year-old daughter. Beau had never disliked him. Had never had a reason to.

Until Noelle had mentioned in passing one morning that Val was going on a second date with him, and he became Beau's number one most disliked person: second only to Wes, Val's cheating ex-husband.

He pushed away from the counter and crossed the small kitchen, opening cupboards until he found the bottle of whiskey she had offered earlier, along with a highball glass. He took it down, uncapped it, and poured a hefty portion into the bottom of the glass before tossing it back in one swallow.

The smart thing to do would be to grab his clothes and retreat to his own apartment.

How was he going to look at her now? See her every day in his coffee shop, now that he knew what she tasted like, what her skin felt like beneath his fingers... what she felt like coming for him, or the way his name sounded on her lips while he was buried inside her? How was he supposed to go back to *before*?

Because all he wanted to do was this same exact thing, every single night, and morning, and *fuck*, during the daytime, too. Anytime she'd want. Any *way* she'd want. He didn't care, as long as he could hear his name fall from her lips while it was his mouth, his fingers, his cock making her come as hard as possible, *as many times* as possible.

So, despite knowing the smart thing to do was to take his leave, he returned to her small bedroom and slid beneath the covers next to her, gathering her against him once again. Beau had never, not once, stayed the night with a woman. He was breaking all kinds of rules tonight. Val sighed in her sleep, burrowing against him and into the pillows, and studiously ignored the way his heart picked up its pace in his chest at just how *good* it felt. He kissed the back of her neck, then closed his eyes, and was asleep in minutes.

CHAPTER 12

*V*al woke by slow degrees. She couldn't remember the last time she'd slept so soundly, or so comfortably. She was warm and though her head ached lightly, she was deliriously cozy. Stretching, her eyes snapped open when she realized why she was so warm; the entire backside of her body was pressed fully against another form, a heavy, warm arm wrapped around her waist. A strong, large hand was nestled in the groove between her breasts, and a long, muscled leg was draped over the back of one of hers.

The night before rushed through her mind. Beau. She had slept with *Beau*.

Barely daring to breathe, let alone move, she lay completely still. The shift in her breathing must have awakened him though because she couldn't stop the gasp from tearing from her lips when she felt him growing hard at her backside. His fingers flexed where they were pressed between her breasts, squeezing one lightly as his arm tightened around her, aligning her more fully against his body.

She felt his mouth press against the slope of her shoulder where it met her back and her breathing hitched up another notch as her hips shifted against his lap, grinding into his morning erection. They both groaned in unison.

"If you ignore it, it will go away eventually," he husked against her skin, where his mouth was still pressed. He made no move to shift away from her, though. They remained silent; her body nestled against his.

"Does this still count as part of the date?" she finally asked on a whisper into the grayish dawn of the room that drifted through the curtains.

His hand slid from between her breasts and pressed, palm flat, against the flatness of her ribcage below her breasts. His fingers stroked downward, over the softness of her belly, to the apex of her thighs. His hardness continued to press against her backside.

"Seeing as neither one of us snuck out of bed to leave, it would be a shame to waste it," he breathed low, his lips still trailing along the skin of her shoulder. His beard tickled her, and she nodded. She was damn near panting.

She parted her thighs with a breathy sigh, allowing his fingers access to her. They strummed lightly, circling her clit and making her gasp sharply, before sinking two fingers inside her. She felt his groan as it reverberated through his chest and into her back.

He rolled away from her then, and she glanced at him over her shoulder. He padded, gloriously naked, into the bathroom, and she took the moment to admire his nakedness. Round, firm butt. Long, thick, muscled thighs that gave way to thick calves and well-kept feet. Infinitely broad shoulders that tapered into a sculpted, hard back. Biceps that begged to have a bite taken out of them. Everything dusted with dark hair... and tattoos. Both arms from the backs of his hands to shoulders were heavily inked, which she'd always known. But the tattoos that covered his legs had been a shock to her system the night before, and she hadn't taken nearly enough time to look at them, too distracted by what he'd been doing to her body to pay attention to much else.

She heard a drawer open in the bathroom and some shuffling,

then the sound of cardboard tearing along a perforated edge. He returned a moment later with a foil packet in his hands, and he quickly ripped it open before sliding the condom on his erection. He was back in the bed behind her a second later, pressing his warm body against her back once more.

Gripping the inside of her thigh with his hand, he lifted it higher and wrapped it around the backside of his hips as he lined himself up at her entrance. Val let out a long, low moan as he slid inside, working his hips in short, slow thrusts until he was buried completely. She felt his forehead fall against her shoulder as he huffed out a half sigh, half groan once he was seated fully inside her.

His palm slid from her thigh to her waist, then pressed his palm flat against her lower abdomen as he began to move. "Christ you're so tight," he groaned against the skin of her back. "You take me so well, Val. So good."

He pounded into her hard from behind, her thigh still thrown over his. His hand moved down, and his fingers found her clit again, circling and strumming as he continued to move inside her. It's like his fingers were magic; it wasn't long before she was clutching at his arm, grinding into him as she began to spasm deep within, her orgasm rocketing through her and making her clamp down on his hammering cock.

His breathing was harsh against the back of her neck as she came around him hard, and then her face was being tipped up, his hand wrapped around the underside of her jaw. Their eyes met over her shoulder, and she panted raggedly. "Beau."

He kissed her hard for just a moment, then released her jaw. She squeaked in surprise when he shifted them so that she was on her belly on the bed, and then he was sliding back inside her, her thighs pressed tightly together by his on either side of them. The position made her tighter and she groaned into the pillow when he slammed in deep, hitting that special spot deep inside. His hands pressed into the mattress on either side of her shoulders, his body held off of her by his arms as his hips continued to piston into hers.

"Beau," she whimpered on a low whine, turning her head and pressing her cheek against the pillow. Her cheeks were flushed, and she was hot all over. "You're going to make me come again."

"Good," came his gravelly response somewhere behind her. She felt his weight shift and then the fingers of his right hand were sliding into the hair at the nape of her neck, pulling tight. It arched her neck, and she bit her lower lip to keep from crying out, but not in pain. He knew just the right amount of pressure to apply to turn that bite of pain into pleasure. "We're nowhere near two dozen yet, Val. Give it to me, sweetheart. I want to feel you come on my dick again."

His fingers left her hair and slid down and around her throat, simultaneously tilting her head back and squeezing lightly. "Oh, fuck," she moaned long and low a heartbeat before her mouth dropped open in a silent cry as she came.

He was pulling orgasms out of her like a goddamned magician. She was ruined.

"That's my girl," he growled from above her, his mouth biting down onto the meaty part of her shoulder where it met with her neck. She shuddered, her orgasm stealing every rational thought from her mind and breath from her lungs as his hips slammed into hers. His thrusts stuttered, and then he came with a hoarse shout, his mouth closing over the spot he'd bitten lightly. "Jesus, you come so good, Val. I've never felt a pussy come so hard around my cock, sweetheart. You fucking squeeze me dry."

Somehow, after everything that had happened in the last twelve hours, she was still able to blush. The filthy whispered words into her ear made heat flood her face and she buried her face in the pillow beneath her. His hand was still wrapped lightly around her throat, and she felt the pressure of his fingers against her throat when she swallowed.

When Beau finally rolled off of her, she turned her head and rested her cheek on her stacked hands as she watched him. He stood from the bed, padding naked into the bathroom as he removed the condom. Heat flooded her cheeks again as he shut the door. Her body was sore, muscles she hadn't used in far too long being put to use; rigorous use.

Propping her chin in her hands, she smiled at Beau as he came out of the bathroom a few minutes later. He was glorious in his nakedness and she looked her fill as he walked back toward the bed. Reaching out, he let his palm crack across her naked butt and she gasped in shock. Laughing, he leaned down to press a kiss to her mouth before straightening again.

"I trust that you have all the fixings for coffee here, or do I need to run downstairs?" he asked, running his hand over the butt cheek he'd just spanked, soothing away the bite of the slap.

She nodded. His fingers squeezed the roundness that filled his palm and he groaned, his eyes leaving hers to follow the trail that his hand was making. "Fuck, this ass. So pretty."

Then he straightened, leaning down to pick up his boxer-briefs that had been tossed aside the night before. Pulling them up his legs, she admired the way his muscles bunched and smoothed out with each move he made. Adjusting himself in his underwear, he winked at her when she raised her eyes back to his before he turned and left the bedroom, walking out into her living room and kitchen wearing nothing but a tight pair of black underwear.

Val groaned and finally rolled out of bed, stepping across the room to the bathroom. Closing the door, she peered at herself in the mirror. Her hair was tousled around her shoulders. Her mouth was kiss-swollen and beard-abraded, and she raised her fingers to touch her lips lightly as she stared. Mascara was smudged beneath her eyes and she groaned. Washing her face hurriedly, she removed all of her slept in make-up and then smoothed her facial moisturizer over her clean skin. Beau had seen her with no make-up a hundred times... but this was different.

They were different.

The floors in her apartment were always stone cold, so she pulled a fuzzy pair of Valentine's themed socks onto her feet. Sliding her arms into a soft pink bathrobe with tiny red hearts all over it, she tied the sash around her waist and then took a deep breath in before stepping out of the bathroom and out the bedroom door.

Beau was standing at her kitchen sink, coffee cup in hand, staring out the small window that looked out over the snow-covered street below. Still wearing nothing but his tight boxer-briefs. His glorious tattooed body on full display.

When she knew he heard her behind him, he turned, and she blushed to the roots of her hair. His gaze swept from the top of her head down to her fuzzy Valentine stockinged toes and then back up until they stopped on hers. "There you are. I was wondering if you were going to hide in there until I got the hint and left."

Val shook her head, stepping forward until she stood directly in front of him. He set his coffee cup on the counter beside them and opened his arms. She sighed and stepped into the circle of his arms, closing her eyes as they closed around her tightly, wrapping her own around his naked torso. Her fingers smoothed over the nakedness of his back. They stood that way for a long time. Far longer than sixty seconds. Finally, she inhaled deeply and released it slowly before whispering against his skin, "Can we just... pretend nothing out there exists? Just for a little longer?" she tightened her arms around his waist. "I'm not ready for you to let go yet. Is that okay?"

CHAPTER 13

S omething tugged viciously at the cold stone in his chest
that was his heart. Smoothing his hand over her hair,
he kissed the crown of her head. "As long as you want,
sweetheart."

She nodded against his chest and he felt her lips moving
across his bare skin. This felt… surprisingly right. Surprisingly
normal.

"Theo and Miles are on shift today," he said quietly, his lips
moving directly against the top of her head.

"They are?" she asked, raising her head so she could look at
him. He nodded. Her eyes crinkled at the corners when she
smiled, and then she returned her cheek to resting against his
chest. "I don't work today, either." She flattened her hands against
the skin of his back and he couldn't stop the smile that tugged at
his mouth. "But I don't want you to think you have to stay, if you
don't want to…"

"Why don't we start with coffee and maybe some breakfast,"
he murmured, smoothing his hands over her back and arms. The
robe she wore was incredibly soft against his palms. He kissed

her forehead, just because he could. Just because, it too, felt right. "And maybe I'll run across the hall and get a change of clothes."

"You don't want to wear your jeans and nice shirt?" she asked, the teasing in her tone belied by the tightening of her arms around his waist.

"I think I'd much rather lounge around in sweats and a t-shirt, but if I have to put my date clothes back on, then so do you. I'm going to have dreams about that dress, Val."

She laughed, the sound vibrating through his own chest and he tightened his arms around her again. "You liked that dress?"

"Sweetheart," he whispered, lowering his lips to her temple, where he pressed another kiss, "that dress was stunning. The memory of you standing in front of me and dropping that dress to the floor... You, my dear Valentina, are what sex fantasies are made of."

Val laughed and raised her head, rolling her eyes at him, before finally stepping away. He loosened his arms, letting them drop to his sides. She glanced down his body and he felt his dick jump, already half hard just thinking about her stripping out of that dress the night before. Or the way she tasted on his tongue. And the way she felt coming for him. Fuck.

He clasped her face between his hands and lowered his mouth to hers, kissing her thoroughly, languidly. He never wanted to stop. "I don't know what kind of voodoo magic you wield, woman."

"I'll never tell," she sing-songed breathily against his lips, smiling.

Finally releasing her, he stepped back and turned toward the coffee maker, pouring a cup and then handing it to her, already lightened with French vanilla creamer from the refrigerator, then topped off his own cup.

"I'm going to run across the hall and grab some clothes, can I trust you to sit and relax with this coffee without doing a classic Val freakout about what happened last night the second I walk out the door?" he asked, taking a sip of his coffee. When she rolled her eyes at him, he scowled down at her over the rim of his cup. "I need the words, Val."

"Yes, I will be fine while you go to your apartment and change clothes. No, I will not freak out."

He narrowed his eyes on her for a moment longer, watching her face for any hint of a lie, but then he said, "Okay. I'll only be gone for a few minutes. I won't even be gone long enough for my coffee to get cold, okay?"

"Yes, Beau," she sighed, rolling her eyes at him again as she leaned her hips against the island counter, holding her coffee cup between her clasped hands, level with her chest.

"Good girl," he murmured and dropped another kiss to her unsuspecting mouth before heading toward the bedroom. Thirty seconds later he was back, jeans on and button-down shirt pulled on but left open, socks and shoes in hand. "I'll be right back, sweetheart."

Letting himself out of her apartment, he strode across the short hallway to his own, unlocking the door quickly and stepping in. He dropped his shoes at the door before heading into his bedroom, tugging the shirt off before he cleared the doorway. Sliding his jeans back down his thighs, along with his underwear, he tossed them and the shirt onto the bed as he stepped toward the dresser. Pulling on a fresh pair of boxer-briefs, he then shoved his feet into a set of dark gray sweatpants, leaving them slung low on his hips, before shoving his arms and head through the holes of a simple white t-shirt. The material clung to his shoulders and biceps, but was loose enough on his torso to be comfortable. He picked up his glasses and contacts case, his eyes already beginning to burn from leaving his contacts in overnight. Lastly, he slid his feet into a well-worn pair of men's slippers—because the hardwood floors in their apartments were chilly—before heading back toward Val's. Stopping at her door, he knocked, but when he heard her call out to come in, he turned the handle and let himself back inside.

He hadn't allowed himself the time to analyze what had transpired between them in the last twelve hours. He didn't want to. For now, this felt right. And he wasn't going to let his own guilty conscience ruin it.

Because Christ... if he let the guilt kick in. It was going to wreck him. Completely.

CHAPTER 14

"Why do you have two sets of the same books?"

"Huh?" Val asked, crossing the room with two plates piled with breakfast sandwiches and fruit toward him. She looked over his shoulder as she got closer, where he stood in front of one of the bookshelves that lined her small living room. He accepted the plate with a thank you and a quick kiss on her mouth, which made her blush, and then he pointed to several books on one shelf. She made a face and bit her lip. "Oh. Those. Uhh…"

Setting her plate down on the coffee table, she stepped up to the bookshelf and pulled two of the books down, both with the same title by the same author, but the covers were different. Holding them up, she let him look at them and she licked her lips, blushing again. On one cover was a man with a button-down shirt left open revealing glistening abs with a cowboy hat pulled low over his face. The other, a beautiful floral cover in shades of aqua.

"*These* are by a new author I just found," she whispered, sliding the books back into their respective spots. She gestured to the others on the shelf. "She's local, and all of her books are based right here in Petoskey. How cool is that? It's called the *Petoskey Stone Series* and they're just... *ugh. So good.* I met her at a signing downtown. And she has the hot man covers, but she does these pretty discreet covers, too... and I just couldn't decide which ones I liked better. So... I have all of them." She shrugged awkwardly. Pointing to another shelf, she continued, "The *Cherry Tree Harbor Series* has hot man covers and discreet covers... so, naturally I had to get both, since she's another Michigan author and all of hers are based in northern Michigan, too. I have multiple versions of the *Salacious Players Club* because she has the original hot man covers that are discontinued so you can't find them anymore, the discreet trad published covers, and the stunning special edition foil covers... I have the special edition foil covers *and* the hot man covers of *The Alliance Series*, too, which are all signed by SJ herself... And I have first edition paperbacks of *ACOTAR* as well as a hardback set with custom dust jackets." Beau was staring down at her. She wrinkled her nose in embarrassment. "It's a disease. Incurable. *Book-Dragon-Itis.*"

Beau burst out laughing, shaking his head as he turned away from the shelves and sank down into one corner of the couch. He set his plate in his lap as she sat down next to him, picking up her plate off the coffee table in front of them. Motioning to the other shelves, he asked, "And you've read all of these?"

"Umm," Val mumbled around a bite of her breakfast sandwich. She chewed and swallowed quickly. Pointing to a shelf on the far side of the room, she said, "That's my TBR shelf."

"TBR?"

She nodded around another bite of sandwich. "Mmhmm. To-Be-Read."

"What's on that shelf?" he asked before taking a bite of his own.

"*Crescent City, Vicious Lost Boys, Dark Olympus*. Among others."

"*Vicious Lost Boys? Dark Olympus?*"

"Yeah." Twisting her legs up underneath her, she sat crisscross applesauce and tugged the edges of the robe over her exposed thighs. Reaching out, she brought her coffee to her lips and took a drink. *If he wants to know...* "The first is a dark, spicy *Peter Pan* retelling. The second is like a... a spicy Greek mythology series. I've read the first few in that series. I need to buy the others still, so I can finish it."

"What are you currently reading?" he asked.

Swallowing hard, she blushed. "Umm. A why choose hockey romance."

"Why choose?"

Oh. My. God. Please let the couch open up and swallow me.

"It means multiple men, one woman," she whispered, face flaming.

Beau nodded, as if this was a totally normal conversation and she hadn't just told him she like to read about a woman being railed by multiple guys at the same time. *No biggie. This is fine.* He popped a bite of melon into his mouth. "Are all of the books you read of the spicy variety?"

She shook her head and took another drink of coffee. *Fuck it. Can't get any worse. Just go for it, Val.* "No, not all of them. But it is my preferred genre, and I am a self-proclaimed expert in Cliterature."

She enjoyed the laugh that rolled out of him, making him throw his head back. "Jesus, Val. Cliterature?"

"Would you rather I just call it smut?" she deadpanned.

"Is this why your light is still on at three am some nights?" he asked, peering at her over the last bite of his sandwich.

"Sometimes," she laughed. "What are *you* doing awake at three am?"

As soon as the question left her mouth, she regretted asking it. She knew what virile, sexy, habitually single bachelors did at three am.

And the thought of Beau with other women made the bite of sandwich she'd just taken turn to ash in her mouth. She swallowed around the lump in her throat and lowered her eyes from his face.

"My day starts at three-thirty," he said gently. "Coffee shop doesn't open at five-thirty on its own."

"You *wake up* at three-thirty? *On purpose?*"

She could feel the astonishment pulling her eyebrows up. Who wakes up that early by choice? Psychopaths, that's who.

He laughed, nodding, as he set aside his plate and picked up his coffee, taking a deep swallow. "I usually hit the gym before I go to work. Or go for a run."

"Yuck," Val laughed, shivering in aversion. "The only thing that I run is my mouth."

Beau laughed out loud again, then murmured huskily, "You seem to prefer a different kind of cardio."

The blush that crept up her neck and stained her cheeks made her face hot. "I do like that kind of cardio."

CHAPTER 15

They had sex on every possible surface in the apartment. Beau made sure that she came... many, many times. On his tongue. His fingers. His dick. Fuck, did he love feeling her come on his dick. She came with her entire body; her thighs shaking, belly quivering, hands scrabbling for any kind of handhold as he tore her apart and stitched her back together one orgasm at a time. He wanted to erase any other man from her mind, her body. Until all that was left was him, them. Together.

"I mean, this is still part of the date, right?" she asked, panting, as he slid inside her. She moaned low in her throat and the sound of it skittered around his spine, making his balls tighten. Fuck, he didn't want to come yet.

"I don't see why it would have to end now," he agreed with a lopsided grin, though his words came out choppy. Dropping his mouth to her throat, he inhaled deeply the scent of her as he continued to rock his hips into hers. "Safe to say this date could very well last all night and into the morning."

"Again."

She smiled at him when he winked, reaching between their bodies to strum his fingers across her clit. "I still have orgasms to gift, my dear Valentina."

He didn't want this to end, but the way her pussy was clenching around him... he was about to blow, and he needed her to come.

"Come on, sweetheart," he whispered on a groan. "Fuck, Val. Come for me. I'm going to—"

Val's hands spread wide over his ass, pulling him tighter against her as she threw her head back and moaned brokenly through the orgasm that rocketed through her. As soon as those first spasms squeezed him, he was done. Slamming into her, he clenched his teeth tight as his own orgasm tore through him, filling up the condom while he was still buried deep. Her inner muscles squeezed the life out of him and he panted raggedly against the soft, fragrant skin of her neck.

He rolled them to their sides and tugged the condom off, tying it and tossing it into the garbage can that had been moved out of the bathroom and closer to the bed. Throwing one arm up over his head, the other tightened around Val's shoulders and tugged her into his side as he panted for breath.

"Fucking Christ, Val. You're a fucking witch."

She laughed lightly, running her fingers over the skin of his abdomen, which tickled and made him clench his muscles against the sensation. She stilled her hand and pressed her palm flat against him, before moving her hand up toward his chest, which was a much safer location for idle petting. Laying entwined, the only sound their slowly calming breathing, he chuckled when he heard the unmistakable sound of her stomach growling.

"Food?"

She nodded against his chest. "Food," she agreed weakly.

They ordered *doordash* Chinese for dinner and ate out of the containers, sitting together in Val's bed propped against the headboard. *Friends* reruns played on the tv across the bedroom. He had tugged on his sweatpants, and she wore only his white t-shirt. His contacts had been removed and he'd put on a pair of thick rimmed black glasses earlier, needing to give his eyes a break from the contact lenses. Val had stared at him when he'd exited the bathroom wearing his glasses, and once he thought about it, he realized she'd never seen him wearing them before. She had admitted shyly that she liked them. A lot. He vowed to wear them around her more often. Especially if it made her look at him with that burning hunger in her gaze. Fuck it was hot.

"I think you've destroyed my lady bits," she mumbled around a bite of lo mien noodles. "I haven't had this much sex... like. Ever. You're some kind of sex god. How are you still going?"

Popping a crab wonton into his mouth, he waggled his dark eyebrows at her, making her laugh. "You really don't understand the effect you have on me, do you?"

Watching her next to him, she shook her head, her hazel eyes never leaving his. Reaching out, he tucked one dark tendril of hair behind her ear. "It's never been like this for me before. Not with anyone."

"Good," he whispered thickly, that primal urge to beat his chest with his fists nearly overwhelming. "This is different for me, too, sweetheart."

And it was. Never had he spent a night with another woman. Never had he stayed well into the next day... and then into the evening. He didn't do meals with the women he hooked up with. Because that's all it was. An exchange of something physical to get him through the every day. Never had he wanted to spend more than a single evening with any of them. He hadn't truly dated in nearly a decade. It was just easier to be alone. No one to depend on him. No one to nag him. No one to pester him on when he'd be home, how late he'd be out, why he was working so much, blah blah blah.

But he wanted to be here with Val. Fuck, he didn't even want to go to work in the morning. For the first time in years, he truly considered calling in 'sick'. Just to play hooky and spend more time with Val. Doing absolutely nothing but exactly this.

CHAPTER 16

"How come you don't date?"

The hands that were lathering her hair with shampoo stilled for just a fraction of a heartbeat before resuming their manipulations. Standing in front of Beau in the shower, her back to his front, they let the hot water beat down on them. With her back to him and her eyes closed, she'd finally dredged up the nerve to ask him.

"I just mean, you're an attractive guy," she continued softly. "And you're always so sweet. Even if you try to hide it with the grumpy old man routine."

One of his hands slid around her neck, tilting her face up and back so that she was looking at him over her shoulder. "Grumpy old man?" he growled, frowning down at her. She laughed and shrugged before reaching up with her mouth to kiss him quickly. He nudged the curve of her ass with his dick, which was half hard at her back. "Do I need to remind you, my dear Valentina, how *not* old and grumpy I am?" Tightening his hand around her throat, she smiled against his lips. "I dare you to look me in the eyes and tell me some wafflenut half my age could do to you what I have in the last two days, sweetheart. You could say the words, but your body doesn't lie."

He was right, the damn jerk. Whatever this was... she'd never experienced sex like this before in her life. And still she wanted more. Beau had awoken something in her and she was beginning to be terrified of when it would end. Because she knew it would. It had to. It was her and Beau. He'd stayed the night again, waking her up in much the same way he had the morning before. Afterward, he'd hopped out of bed and started coffee, bringing two steaming cups into the bedroom before hauling her out of bed and into the shower with him. She liked having him here. She didn't want it to end. Which brought her back to her question...

"So why don't you date?" she asked again. "If you're so talented... why haven't you settled down to give some lucky lady the privilege of *Orgasms by Beau* for the rest of her days?"

"Because I'm a grumpy old cuss that doesn't like the idea of sharing my time or my space with anyone else."

"So, you do admit to being a grumpy old man?" she teased, leaning back as he used the shower head to rinse her hair of the shampoo. "There's no one that has made you want that? Don't you ever get lonely?"

She felt him shrug behind her and heard his heavy inhale and exhale. "I'm too old for all that, Val. I think that ship sailed a long time ago."

She heard a cap snap behind her, and then his fingers were smoothing the conditioner through her shoulder length hair before rinsing it clean. Everything that he did... it didn't make sense. He was so sweet and attentive. He'd always been different with her. Hadn't he?

Sighing quietly, he brushed her hair over one shoulder and ducked to press a kiss to the curve of her shoulder. "I'm not good company most of the time, sweetheart."

"I don't believe that," she said softly, leaning back against his chest. Reaching behind her, she grabbed his hands and pulled them around her, so that his arms banded around her waist. Holding both of his hands in hers against her stomach just beneath her breasts, she sighed when he rested his chin over her shoulder. "I think you could make someone really happy, Beau. You deserve to be happy, too. Happiness isn't just for everyone else."

The thought of him being with someone else made her chest ache, like her heart was being trampled beneath her breastbone. This was why she didn't do casual hookups. She caught feelings too quickly... and it didn't help that Beau had always had a special piece of her heart, anyway.

Sadness crept in. This isn't what was supposed to happen. They were supposed to go on a date. A *fake* date. A *fake date* that was supposed to end clean and tangle-free... instead she'd kissed him, begged him to stay, to sleep with her... and her dumb-self had gone and caught feelings. Stupid, stupid feelings. For a man that she knew would never reciprocate. Self-proclaimed bachelor, or had she forgotten?

Way to go, Val. Can't even do a fake date or one night stand right. Ugh. Pathetic.

His hand drifted down to the junction of her thighs, and she tipped her head back against his shoulder when his fingers slid between her legs. "I haven't been as happy in years as I have been between these thighs, sweetheart," he whispered huskily against her ear. She moaned when his fingers slipped inside her, pressing deep. One finger, then two. Her knees threatened to buckle. "You've got all the happiness I need right here. Let me find my happy, Val."

That... shouldn't have been as hot as it was. But she exalted in his words; because she, Val, was enough to drive Beau Collins crazy. Was enough to make him happy... at least for now. She felt powerful. Sexy. Desired. He did all those things for her and she wasn't going to deny him or herself anything that felt this good. Not now, at least.

He turned her roughly, slamming her back against the cool tile of the shower and she gasped from the cold against her skin before his mouth closed over hers, silencing the gasp. And then she was being lifted, his hands gripping the meaty part of her hips. Her arms circled his neck, resting them on his shoulders as he pinned her against the wall. His hands dug into the curves of her ass at the same time she wrapped her legs around his waist, the head of his dick poised at her entrance.

"Fuck."

He pressed his forehead against her shoulder and panted, but didn't move, and didn't enter her.

She wiggled in his arms, searching. He growled in her ear, "Stop, Val."

"Why?" she moaned, circling her hips again. "What's wrong?"

"I don't have a condom on."

"Beau. I trust you. I haven't been with anyone but you in two years. I'm clean. Please," she whined, pressing her mouth to his neck. "Please."

"God dammit, Val," he snarled before he pulled her down on his length, seating himself inside her fully. Bare.

"Ohmygod," she moaned loudly, dropping her head back against the shower wall. With nothing between them... he felt so good inside her. So right. "Yes, please."

Using his arms, he raised and lowered her on his length again and again, pulling her up nearly to the tip before slamming her back down on him. He was so deep, hitting that spot that only he seemed able to find.

"What are you doing to me?" he whispered brokenly against her temple as he continued to hammer into her. "Why can't I get enough of you?"

She wasn't sure he meant for her to hear him; he was whispering the words so quietly. The raw emotion in his voice almost undid her. Because she was wondering the same thing.

"I don't want this to end," she whispered back, turning her face so that her lips were nearly at his ear. She was so close to coming, could feel it as her inner muscles began to spasm around him. "I don't want you to let go."

"Fuck, I don't want to," he groaned brokenly as his hips began to stutter. "I don't want to let go either, sweetheart."

"Beau, come with me, please—"

"I'm right here, sweetheart. Come for me," he gritted out, and then she was coming, detonating around him, at the same time she could feel every spurt of his own release deep inside. She cried out when he bit down sharply on the meaty part of her shoulder where it met her neck as they came together. When he set her down, their legs were trembling, and their breathing was labored. Pressing his mouth to hers again, he panted reverently, "*Val.*"

"I know..."

It was all she could say, her throat too thick with emotion to allow anything else. She pressed another kiss to his lips, just a meeting of their mouths, gentle and tentative and chaste. His hands slid up her shoulders to bracket either side of her head, fingers threaded through her wet hair at the back of her head, holding her still. They simply breathed together, mouths meeting in sipping kisses, over and over again, before he sighed and leaned away, smiling down at her.

He slapped one of her butt cheeks with the palm of his hand lightly, then squeezed. "Go on, I'll be out in a minute."

Grinning from ear to ear, she left Beau in the shower and stepped out. Drying off with a fluffy white towel, she then wrapped it around her body just as she heard a sharp knock on her door. A half a heartbeat later, she heard the quiet, unmistakable groan of the old door opening, and then, "Val?"

Val gasped and rushed from the bathroom, pulling the door so that it was mostly closed in her haste. Skidding to a stop in the doorway of her bedroom, she gave Noelle a weak smile where she stood in the entryway. "Hey."

"Urgh, it smells like sex in here." Noelle made a face and then her features went blank, her eyes finally going wide with horror. "Oh my god! Oh my *god*—"

"*Shhh!*" Val hissed, taking a step forward, then she heard the shower shut off. Noelle's eyes flashed to the doorway behind Val and Val cringed slightly as she rushed forward.

"*He's still here?!*" Noelle shrieked, her voice going up an octave. "Oh my god! Is it Beau?!"

Grimacing, she nodded. "Yes, it's Beau."

"Val, it's been *two days*! Wait, is this why he called in 'sick' to work today?! Because y'all are busy *doing the diddly*—"

"Would you *shut up*?!" Val hissed again, reaching out and slapping a hand over her sister's mouth while clasping the towel closed tightly with the other. She glanced behind her at the still open bedroom door. She prayed Beau wouldn't walk out of the bathroom naked... they'd spent most of the last two days wearing little to no clothing. "I'm not sure everyone downstairs heard you!"

"'dis ish 'ucking aweshom—" Noelle mumbled from behind Val's hand, still clasped over her mouth. Her green eyes were twinkling with mischief. Val rolled her eyes and shoved her back toward the door. "Get iht, 'al!"

"Go away!" Val hissed, laughing despite herself, finally releasing her sister's mouth and reaching behind her to grab the door handle and swing it open. Her other hand still firmly holding the towel in place.

Noelle sidestepped out the door onto the landing but shouted as Val was closing the door, "—I want *details*, woman! *Details!*"

The door shut on Noelle and Val sighed as she leaned back against the heavy door. She could hear her sister's cackling laughter as she plodded down the stairs. Beau exited the bedroom, wearing a clean pair of sweatpants. He was pulling a white t-shirt over his head, his hair still damp where it lay on his forehead, tousled from the towel. His glasses were back on, and they did something to her belly.

Val's face pulled into a chagrined half grin, half grimace from where she remained leaning against the door. "I think we've been discovered."

He snorted a laugh and padded across the room to the kitchen, where he poured another cup of coffee. "I'd say that's a safe assumption."

"I'm sorry. I didn't think she'd come up here unannounced."

He shrugged, his shoulder muscles bunching and releasing beneath the thin material of the t-shirt with the movement. "It's just sex, Val. Everyone does it."

The words were innocent enough... And they were true. But the tone of his voice made Val's eyebrows pull into a V, while her throat closed with anxiety. They were clipped and formal, so unlike the emotion-fraught moments from the bathroom just minutes prior.

"Right..." Stepping away from the door, she crossed the room and said quietly, not trusting her voice not to shake, "I'm just gonna go get dressed..."

He nodded once, not looking at her, and her chest ached. This was it; she knew. He was pulling away from her, just like she always knew he would. Because this was *just sex*, after all.

When she came out of the bedroom a few minutes later, she was dressed in a pair of olive-green jogger pants that were banded at her ankles and a cropped gray sweater that hung off one shoulder, revealing one strap of the sports bra she'd pulled on. She'd clipped half of her hair back into a claw clip, the bottom half left out to dry in waves against her neck.

He had gathered his stuff; his glasses and contacts cases, the sweatpants he'd worn the day before piled on the edge of the counter, and his slippers were on his feet. He came around the kitchen island and dropped a chaste kiss to the corner of her mouth. She hated it.

"I should head home," he said, and even though she knew it was coming, it still hurt. Really, really bad. "I called in this morning, but I should probably go in to relieve Theo."

"Oh. Okay... Sure," she said, her voice cracking. She swallowed hard. Unable to meet his eyes, she just nodded, staring at the base of his throat. "I mean, of course."

She wanted to wrap her arms around him and tell him not to go. She wanted to beg him *not to let go*, because she wasn't ready. She wasn't ready for him to let go.

But she didn't have the courage to do it. Couldn't bring herself to raise her arms to wrap them around him, couldn't force the words to come out of her mouth. He had always been a safe place for her. Someone she could go to no matter what. She could count on him to hold her and not let go until she was ready. She didn't even have to ask most of the time. He just *knew*. But now, she didn't want him to do it because she had to ask for it. Tears stung her nose and she blinked rapidly to dispel them from her eyes before he could see them.

The realization hit her like a blow to the chest. He hadn't wanted *her*. He'd done it out of pity, because she'd asked. No, she had *begged*; and he had done exactly what she asked for, because he was Beau and he couldn't tell her no.

"Thanks for the fake date," she whispered as bravely as she could, trying to force a little levity into her tone and doing her best to lift her lips into a smile. She felt her lips wobbling from unshed tears almost immediately. Stepping around him, she headed toward the coffee machine just to give her hands something to do, something for her to look at other than the man that had in just two days destroyed what was left of her heart. "I'll uh... I'll see you, Beau."

Stupid, stupid woman.

"Right," she heard him say, and out of the corner of her eye watched as he picked up his things, cradling them in one arm. "See you, Val."

Val remained stock still until she heard the click of her door close as he let himself out before she let the first tears fall.

CHAPTER 17

*B*eau forced his feet to move away from her door, even as the sound of her crying tore him to shreds. Every last little bit of him lay shattered at his feet.

Guilt so strong it made his stomach revolt ate at him mercilessly. This dead weight in his chest—which he assumed was his traitorous heart that after nearly forty years had finally decided to start working—made it feel like he was dying. Maybe he was.

This is why he didn't do feelings. Fucking hell.

He let himself into his apartment and set his things down on the counter. It was so similar to Val's apartment, but she'd made hers feel homey, where his still felt stark... and dammit was she right but it felt *lonely*.

He rubbed at his chest in an effort to dispel the torturous ache that had taken up residence beneath his breastbone. Was this a heart attack? Nothing should feel like this.

But no, he wasn't in cardiac arrest nor was he suffering from heartburn.

He had spent two days in bed with Val. Two days and two nights of non-stop orgasmic, marathon sex. The kind he'd never experienced... and he had experienced *a lot* of sex in his bachelor driven life.

Two days was all it took for him to fall absolutely, irrevocably, truly and madly in love with Valentina Compton.

What the actual fuck.

When the realization had hit him in the shower, when the truth of the depth of his feelings for Val surfaced and threatened to choke him, the overwhelming guilt that had assailed him had nearly brought him to his knees.

As a kid, he'd spent a lot of time with his dad and Hank. The two were best friends, you never found one without the other, and then he joined as the oldest son between the two friends. Hank and Rachel had not had any sons, so as he'd grown, he'd become a sort of adopted son to Hank. Whether his dad and Hank were out having a garage beer, playing horseshoes in the backyard, going ice-fishing, he was always added to the mix.

He had felt Hank's death as acutely as his father did. They'd both lost a best friend, and he had lost a secondary father/uncle figure.

When Hank knew his time was coming, he'd pulled Beau aside and asked him to watch over his girls, all four of them. He had promised he would, even as the reality had set in that this great man would soon be gone. And he had followed through on that promise. He always would.

Would Hank feel betrayed by him, if he knew what had happened between himself and Val this weekend? Beau couldn't imagine that fucking his eldest daughter into oblivion was what Hank had in mind when he asked him to take care of his girls.

But fuck... the way she'd looked in that dress. The way she'd looked stepping *out* of that dress... He would never get that out of his head. The way her body was so receptive and how responsive she was to his touch; it was like she had been made for him. This was why nothing else had felt right. Why nothing else had ever made him want to settle down. They fit together. Hadn't they always?

Is that why Hank had asked Beau to watch over them? Because he knew, somehow, that this is exactly where he and Val would end up? Hadn't Rachel been hinting at it for years and he just brushed it off as a mother's worry for her daughter and an extension of worry to him as a sort of extra son she'd never had with Hank?

No, there's no way that this is what they'd meant. *Hey, Hank, hope you don't mind I've fucked your daughter against every surface in her apartment, wrapped my fingers around her throat, and made her come with the explosiveness of a freight train... We're good, right? No hard feelings?*

A strangled sort of sound escaped from his throat, and he leaned his hands against the counter, hanging his head between them until his chin nearly touched his chest.

And when the guilt gave way to paralyzing fear, he'd done what he did best. Shut down. Became a dick. Left her with questions in her eyes and dammit if he hadn't wanted to wrap her in his arms and not fucking let go. He'd prayed with every fiber of his being for her to not ask, because if she had, he wouldn't have had the strength to leave.

She deserves better, he thought miserably, staring at the wood floor between his slipper clad feet. *Better than a quick two-day sex fest and an emotionally stunted nearly forty-year-old man. She deserves the men in her books... Her own personal Prince Charming.*

And Beau would never be that man.

CHAPTER 18

❧

"Why do you look like someone just ran over your puppy?"

"I don't have a puppy."

"Well, if you did, and it just got ran over, this is what it would look like," Theo muttered, waving at Beau's face from where they stood behind the counter of the coffee shop.

Beau grunted and turned away, sinking down into a crouch to re-organize the shelf below; a shelf that definitely didn't need to be re-organized... again. For the third time that morning.

"You gonna share with the class why you've been a real dick the last few days?" his brother asked as he leaned his hips against the back counter.

"Theo."

"Yeah?"

"Fuck off."

"No can do, big brother."

"Then you're fired," Beau snapped, standing and striding down the narrow aisle behind the counter toward the back stock room, carrying a mostly empty box of sugar packets.

Theo's chuckle grated on every last nerve he had left. Val had avoided the coffee shop for several days, sending Noelle or Willow in to get their usual morning orders. He didn't blame her. He was an asshole.

Returning to the front, he glared at Theo, but it did no good. His damn brother was a giant pain in his ass. Had been all week. Pouring a cup of coffee, he took a long swallow, relishing the burn as it traveled down his throat. His own penance for what he'd done.

Through the frosted windows, a flash of dark hair under a pink knitted hat was the only warning he had before the door opened and she walked in.

She stalled just inside, her eyes meeting his for a fraction of a second before lowering to the floor. His heart was hammering in his chest as she came forward, stopping just in front of himself and Theo.

"Good morning," Theo murmured, when it became obvious Beau wasn't going to greet her. "How's our man hating Val today? We are still man hating, right?"

Beau fought the urge to cringe. If only his brother knew the validity of those words. He kept his face impassive as she raised her eyes to Theo for a moment before turning her gaze to his.

He couldn't stand the hurt on her face; in those hazel eyes he knew so well. So, as the emotionally stunted idiot that he was, he stayed obstinately silent, hands shoved into the front pockets of his jeans.

She swallowed hard before dropping her gaze from his. It did nothing to help him breathe any easier. In fact, it only made it worse. Fuck he was an asshole.

"I'll just have our usual," she said quietly to Theo, who side-stepped into Beau to get him to move. Tapping the screen, he typed in the girls' orders.

Val extended her credit card to him, but Beau muttered, his voice a low grunt, "Put that away. On the house."

Snapping her eyes up to his, he saw a flash of fire in her eyes.

Pushing the card toward Theo, she bit out, "No, thank you. I don't need any more of your pity handouts."

He felt his brows pull low over his eyes in a deep scowl as they stared at each other.

"Go ahead and scowl all you want," she muttered, then accepted her card back from Theo, replacing in her purse. He could see her hand trembling. Fucking god dammit. "You can't bully me into taking anything else from you."

"So, fully man hating today, I love it," Theo chuckled with an appreciative nod as he turned away to start the three coffee drinks. "You gonna do something useful or just stand there glaring at her, Beau?"

"Didn't I fucking fire you?" he snapped under his breath as he turned and stalked away from the two of them, rounding the corner into the stock room.

"Geesh, grumpy old man," he heard Theo mutter and then Val's scoff of laughter.

Shoving the fingers of one hand through his hair, he let his head fall back so that he was staring at the ceiling. Taking deep, controlled breaths in, he waited until he was certain she had left before exiting the stock room.

"*So.*"

"Fucking don't, Theo. I mean it," Beau snarled, glaring at his brother again.

He watched out of the corner of his eye as his brother's shoulders rose and fell in a shrug, holding out his hands in an innocent gesture.

"Just strange seeing you two at each other's throats."

"Leave it alone, Theo..."

"Ever since Valentine's Day and that date you two went on..."

"Theo! Seriously, mind your own fucking business!" he snapped. Thankfully the coffee shop was mostly empty, and no one heard them over the sound of the music playing overhead.

Theo pointed at the door, where Val had disappeared through

back out onto the street. "Those girls are my business. Just like they're yours. You think you have a monopoly on caring about them? Just because you were like an extra son to Hank, doesn't mean you're the only one that can give a shit about them. So yeah, when it looks like her heart is fucking breaking all over again, damn right I'm going to ask what the hell happened. So, what the hell happened, Beau?"

"Nothing."

"Really? You've been a fucking ornery cuss all week and she looks like her heart has been torn out and stomped on—"

"Fucking *god dammit*, Theo! Don't you think I could see that?"

"So, what did you do?" Theo demanded, jabbing a finger into his chest. Beau growled and took a step toward his brother. He watched as Theo swallowed hard as realization dawned. Beau turned away and leaned his palms against the counter, staring out over the coffee shop. "You didn't."

"Stop." The word came out as a plea. Of course his brother didn't listen.

"You did. Holy fucking shit," Theo breathed. "Big bad bachelor Beau fell in love. With *Val*."

"I said stop," Beau snarled, turning his head toward his brother.

Theo laughed. Threw his head back and laughed. Beau had never wanted to hit his brother as badly as he did in that moment. Wanted to drop his shoulder and sack him right in the gut like a damn lineman.

"This is fucking *gold*," Theo continued, chuckling still. "So... you two do it?"

"*Fuck off*," he growled again. He was getting the beginning of a headache. Pinching the bridge of his nose between his thumb and forefinger, he sighed heavily. "And don't fucking talk about her like that."

"You totally did," Theo laughed, dancing away when Beau swiped an arm out. "How was it?"

"Theo," Beau snapped, leveling his brother with a furious stare. "*I said enough.*"

"Okay, okay," Theo said, holding his hands up in surrender. "Understood."

Beau straightened and turned to take a drink of his coffee.

"Can I ask why she looked ready to cry when she walked in here though? Did you not make her come? Not every guy can, it's totally normal for a guy your age to have performance issues man—"

Beau lunged for Theo, but the younger man danced away on the balls of his feet again, laughing, before he took off into the back stock room to hide from a furious Beau.

CHAPTER 19

"*A*lright, enough."

Val looked up from her laptop, where she was sitting in the back room of *Three Blossom* crunching numbers from the holiday the week before. Her brows drew into a frown when her sisters surrounded her. Noelle's arms were crossed over her chest, one hip thrown out for balance. Willow had her hands shoved into the front pocket of her giant *Lake Michigan, Unsalted and Shark Free* hoodie, her face screwed up into one of worry.

"What?" Val asked, straightening from where she was hunched over the laptop.

"I can't handle the sad, mopey Val for another day. I want my sister back, dammit," Noelle snapped, uncrossing her arms and letting them fall to her sides, where her palms slapped against her jean clad thighs.

"Sad and mopey?" Val asked.

"Yes. I don't know what happened between Sunday and Monday, but something happened. You refuse to go into *Beau's*. You refuse to talk about your date, or anything that happened afterward. When I saw you Sunday morning you were... I don't know. Happy. You looked like the old Val for a minute. What happened?" Noelle demanded, stepping up closer to the steel counter opposite where Val sat.

"It was a fake date. A fake weekend. That's all that it was, and now it's done," Val said, trying her best to make her voice not quiver. When Noelle opened her mouth to protest, Val raised one hand, palm out to stop her. "It's done, Noe. He made that very clear."

"I refuse to believe that," her sister said, shaking her head in denial. Val heaved a sigh and closed the laptop. She wouldn't be getting anything else done. Pointing with one finger toward the wall that separated *Three Blossom Haven* from *Beau's* next door, she continued, "Because that man is just as much of a wreck over there as you are."

"That's ridiculous," Val snorted, shaking her head as she stood from the stool she had been perched on. Rounding the steel worktable, she headed to the front of the store. "He's the one that just shut down out of the blue..." Memories of how he'd been in the shower moments before everything had changed, like a switch being flipped took over her mind, and she shook her head again to clear it. No, she wouldn't' think about that. Not now. Straightening her shoulders, she turned to find Noelle and Willow had followed her. "He hasn't talked to me in over a week and a half, other than our run in at the coffee shop the other morning. He made it clear what happened was over. It meant nothing."

Noelle was already shaking her head again. "No. There's no way it was nothing. You haven't seen Beau for the last week and a half. It's like... Ugh, I don't know. He's always been a grumpy fucker, but now he's just... awful. I don't think he's nearly as unaffected as you seem to think he is."

"Yeah, well, he certainly knows how to find me, and yet he hasn't," Val snapped bitterly. They lived across the hall from one another, for heaven's sake! They worked next door to each other, every single day! "He said he's always going to be a bachelor. He's not going to settle down, he's not dating material, and he's certainly never going to get married. I won't settle for someone that doesn't want the whole thing. I wasted too many years with someone that was never going to want to go the long haul with me. Don't I deserve that? Don't we all deserve that kind of love?"

Willow sighed and stepped closer to her. "Do you really think that the kind of love you read about in your books is out there? In real life?"

"Yes," Val whispered immediately, without hesitation. She believed it with everything that was inside of her. "Yes, I do. And dammit, that's what I want."

"A tall, dark haired, bearded, heavily tattooed lumberjack—er, *coffeehouse owner*—"

"No, that's not what I'm saying—"

"Puh-lease. You're so head over heels in love with Beau, even Theo with his one brain cell can see it," Noelle muttered, rolling her eyes.

"I'm not in love with Beau," Val whispered, though her heart started thudding in her chest at the blatant lie. When her sisters simply glared at her, she said sadly, "I'm not."

But the truth was, that of course she was in love with Beau. Hadn't she always been? Isn't that why it had been so easy to ask him to kiss her? To stay? Because it was *Beau*.

Beau, who was always there for her. Always. No matter what.

Beau, who gave the best, longest, steadiest hugs in the history of a hug.

Beau, so handsome and sexy and dear lord, the giver of the best orgasms in the entire world.

She hadn't felt as beautiful and desirable as she had with him, possibly ever. He made her feel wanted, but he made her feel safe to be herself, too. With all of her quirks and baggage, he'd never made her feel like a burden, like Wes had.

He remembered the small things that no one else had ever

bothered to pay attention to. She wanted him. Wanted all of him. Wanted to have the chance to give whatever they'd discovered a go. She did.

But she wouldn't beg, or ask, not again. He would have to come to her. She wouldn't sit around waiting for him, either.

CHAPTER 20

"Good morning, Noelle," Beau said when she stepped up to the counter. He raised an eyebrow when she simply crossed her arms and glared at him. Tilting his head to the side, he narrowed his eyes slightly. "The usual, I'm assuming?"

"You're a giant dickhead, you know that, right?"

Inhaling deeply, he looked away from her, glancing at the woman standing behind her. The woman's eyes were wide, bouncing from his to the back of Noelle's head in shock. "Are you going to order? I have a line, Noe."

"Yes, I want the usual. It doesn't change the validity of my statement," she snapped, slapping her palms down onto the counter between them and leaning forward onto her stiff arms. "You're a dickhead. And I don't appreciate you breaking my sister's heart by ignoring her."

Beau tapped the screen and entered the usual order, then pressed the cash button before Noelle could offer payment. The headache that he'd been fighting for several days was back. In the form of a pissed off brunette this time instead of a blonde-haired idiot brother.

"She deserves the world, Noelle. And I can't be the one to give it to her," he said simply, keeping his voice low to avoid anyone in the line behind her from hearing. "I *can't* give it to her."

"Why? Why not, Beau? I've never met two people so miserable trying to stay away from each other as you two!" she hissed, following him along the counter as he walked away to pour their coffees. "And you're right, she does deserve the world. She wants you."

Miles stepped into the spot he'd vacated, taking over orders, so he continued down the counter until they were far enough away from other customers to speak privately. Leaning on his hands on the counter, he sighed. "I'm not what she wants. She wants Prince Charming. I'm not him."

"No, Prince Charming would have swooped in and carried her away, instead of being an ass and pretending she doesn't exist," Noelle muttered sourly. When he nodded in agreement, she rolled her eyes. "I'll say this once. Get your head out of your ass and realize what you've got before it goes away for good. Because you're right, she does deserve the world, but she wants you in that world, for whatever reason that I can't understand right now because I want to punch you in your stupid face so badly I can't see straight. She's a great person and I thought you knew that... but you're just like all the other douchebags she went on dates with in the last four months. Only instead of just wounding her pride, you broke her heart. And I don't know that I can forgive you for that."

Grabbing up the coffee carrier with the three travel coffees tucked into it, she turned and stalked off. But then she stopped and turned around, coming back to stand directly in front of him again. He raised his eyes to hers.

"She has a date for her birthday tomorrow. Do with that information what you will."

Staring after her, he let her words sink in, cutting him deeply. She was already going on a date? With someone new?

Fuck that.

At two o'clock, he left Miles and Theo in charge for the evening and walked the few blocks down to one of the local bookstores in the downtown district. Gold letters painted across the wide window read *Turn The Page* and he pushed open the door. Two women stood on opposite sides of a small wooden counter, one side lined with the week's new arrival and the other filled with individually wrapped baked goods.

"Hi, welcome. Is there anything we can help you find today?" one of them asked, a short, petite brunette with vivid sapphire blue eyes. Her impossibly curly hair was loose around her shoulders and down her back. The other woman, a blonde with shoulder length blonde hair and red rimmed glasses smiled at him from the other side of the counter. Bright red lipstick painted her lips, and she wore an AC/DC band tee.

"I'm looking for a couple books. I don't know the names of them or who the author is. Something about spicy Greek mythology?" he said, stepping forward. Rows and rows of bookshelves towered through the small shop.

The blonde nodded. "There are a few options. Want us to show you and see if anything rings a bell?"

"Yes, please," he said, following both women as they turned down a row, between two of the towers of shelves. They stopped in front of a selection and the brunette pointed out a few.

"This is the *Hades and Persephone Saga*." He glanced at the covers and shook his head, not recognizing the artwork on the covers. "Umm, *Lore of Olympus*? That's more fantasy."

His eyes widened and he snapped his fingers and said, *"Dark Olympus."*

The brunette smiled and reached for another selection. "All of them are right here. Are you looking for any in particular?"

"The last two, whichever those ones are," he said, smiling, too.

"Perfect," the brunette said and plucked two off the shelf, handing them to him. "Anything else we can help you find?"

"No, just these for now." He followed her back to the front of the store, where he placed them on the counter for her to ring them up. She packaged them neatly into brown paper, sealing them with a sticker, before tucking them into a brown paper bag embossed with the store logo. Holding the bag out to him, he took it. "Thank you."

"Hope she loves them," the blonde called as he walked away.

He nodded and grinned. "She will."

CHAPTER 21

⬥

$\mathcal{U}$nlocking the front door, she stepped inside, arms full of groceries. Hauling them to the kitchen island, she huffed as she hoisted them up, setting them down none too gently. It was dark outside, and with her hands full, she couldn't flip the lights on. A single streetlamp across the street shining through the small kitchen window was all the light that was afforded.

Through the darkness of the kitchen, she could just see the pint of Cherry Garcia as it rolled out of one bag and toppled off the counter and onto the floor, thudding dully. She barely caught the bottle of wine before it went the same direction, with a much messier fate than the frozen treat.

Netflix. Cozy socks. A big fluffy blanket. Ice cream. Popcorn. Wine. Comfort movie.

What a crazy birthday night this was going to be. Thirty-three was looking *pretty intense*.

Rolling her eyes, Val scoffed to herself. She'd told Noelle she had a date tonight, just to keep her sisters from breaking down her door and inserting themselves into her evening. She didn't want to people tonight. She just wanted to wallow and binge swoony rom coms. Alone.

Reaching out, she finally flipped the light on in the kitchen and froze.

A giant bouquet of vivid pink peonies, white roses, and sunshiny yellow freesias sat in the center of her counter. Next to it was a neatly wrapped rectangular package with pink, yellow, and white ribbon. A pink envelope sat perched on top, leaning against the flower vase.

She picked up the card, her hand shaking when she recognized Beau's messy scrawl across the front. Opening it, she read the simple Happy Birthday, then her eyes lowered to the bottom of the card.

To add to your book-dragon collection.

Opening the gift, she found the two books, the ones she had mentioned to him that she still needed to finish the series. A slip of paper fell out of one of them and fluttered to the floor as she thumbed through it, and she bent down to pick it up.

Even if you're on a date with another man,
your body will always know it belongs to me.
Even if it started as a fake date,
we both know it wasn't, sweetheart.

"Oh, you arrogant, slimy motherfucker—"

Stomping across the floor, books still clutched in her hands, she wrenched the door open and slammed it closed behind her, striding across the landing toward his door. Raising her fist, she pounded on the heavy wooden door of his apartment. She knew he was home. Could see the thin strip of light from beneath the door. She slammed the flat of her palm against the door again. She was *livid*. How *dare* he— And who was he to get jealous of a date? A date that she had made up, but that was beside the point—

The door swung open, and she looked up into his face, into those impossibly dark chocolate brown eyes. His expression was impassive, as seemed to be his usual now whenever he looked at her. Shoving the books into his chest, she barely made him budge, the big dumb brute, and she snapped, "You know what, fuck you, Beau! I didn't need your pity date because of some ridiculous promise you made to my dad, and I certainly didn't need your pity fuck! Or your stupid books! And—and why would you care if I'm going on a date?!"

"You think I slept with you out of pity? I doubt that's what he meant when he asked me to take care of his girls. And the date? Yeah, *you're not going*," he snarled, yanking the books out of her hands and tossing them onto the floor behind them. She opened her mouth to protest, but he laced his fingers through the back of her hair roughly and she gasped, her mouth moving against his where he was pressed so close. "That fucking promise I made to Hank was the last thing on my mind that night or any time after that, Val, and trust me when I say this never would have happened if it were Noe or Willow. All I could fucking think about was how stunning you looked in that fucking dress and how exquisite you were out of it... How good you felt beneath me, around me... How fucking hard you came on my tongue, my fingers, my dick. The sounds that came out of your mouth while I fucked you... No, Val. The only thing I could think about was you. How I wanted to do exactly that every goddamn night and morning for the rest of my life. And I'll say it again, you're not going on any fucking date with anyone but me."

He kissed her, hard. His tongue snaked into her mouth, and he drank in the moan that escaped her. He pressed his muscled arm around her waist, pulling her closer against his body until she felt how hard he was against her.

"You can't just tell me I'm not allowed to go on a date—" she whispered heatedly but was cut off by another kiss.

"I can and I just did," he growled menacingly, making her shiver. "Cancel on the fucker, Val."

"You avoided me for two weeks," she whispered against his mouth, not responding to the last part. "Why should I cancel my birthday date for someone that didn't talk to me for two weeks?"

Turning her head slightly by tugging her hair, he lowered his mouth to the curve of her throat, where it met her shoulder. He dragged his mouth over her skin hotly, sipping kisses until her entire body broke out in goosebumps.

"I won't lie and say that guilt wasn't eating me alive," he murmured hoarsely against her skin before raising his head to stare at her with those dark eyes. "Your father trusted me to take care of you. I felt like I betrayed that, especially because I enjoyed it so much and never wanted to stop. And I know you don't want to go out with some prick tonight, sweetheart. I know you better than that."

Sighing against his mouth, she kissed him before whispering, "There is no date, Beau. I only told Noelle I had a date so she would leave me to myself tonight. There isn't anyone else."

"You're fucking trouble," he breathed, shaking his head with a low chuckle. "Do you have any idea how insanely jealous I've been since yesterday? Imagining you wearing a dress like you wore for me for some other lousy fucker? I hated it, Val." He swallowed hard then, and she watched his Adam's apple dip in his throat before climbing again. "You deserve the world, sweetheart, and I've been a self-proclaimed bachelor my entire life. Dating isn't something I do, isn't something I even know *how* to do."

Her heart hammered in her chest, and she felt humiliation roil through her. She nodded as tears stung her nose. "Of course," she whispered, lowering her eyes before he could see the tears well in them. *I'm such a fucking idiot! He's already told you all this! Why can't you just take a stupid hint?!*

"I'll screw up more than I get right, especially at first," he continued, his voice gruff. She snapped her head up, her wide eyes meeting his in surprise. His dark eyes crinkled lightly at the corners as he smiled ruefully, at the same time he stroked his thumb over her cheek, over her lower lip. "I'm not good at date nights, or communicating my feelings, or having someone else in my space... But if you'll let me try, I'll always take you to the bookstore and let you get as many damn books as your arms can carry, even if you already have three of the same book. I'll make sure your favorite ice cream is in the freezer, I'll never end a hug until you're ready to let go, and if your body can handle it, I'll give you two dozen orgasms every night." She laughed out loud, her mouth quirking into a bemused smirk. She tilted her cheek into his palm as he cupped it gently, his dark eyes searching hers. "Be mine, Val. You were my first Valentine... I think I'd like you to be my last, if you'll have me, too."

Wrapping her arms around him, he did the same, fitting their bodies as closely together as physically possible. Leaning up, she pressed her mouth to his, sweetly, gently. "Beau?"

"Yeah, Val?" he whispered against her mouth.

"Don't let go."

The smile that curved his lips against hers made her heart ache in the best way possible, and a matching smile tugged at her lips. "Never again, sweetheart. I promise."

EPILOGUE

*S*itting at one of the umbrella covered patio tables outside of *The Wine Garden*, Val watched as the August sun began to set across the bay. The heat of the day had finally started to abate, just enough to be comfortable. A glass of wine sat in front of her, and a waiter came by to clear her salad plate from the table, as well as to refill Beau's draft beer.

Raising the frosty glass, he held it out to her and she smiled, lifting her wine glass to clink it against his. "To the first six months of the rest of our lives, sweetheart."

"You know, for someone that claimed to not be good at this dating thing, you're kinda killin' it, babe," she teased, smiling broadly.

"Yeah?" he asked, not at all attempting to cover the obvious fish for compliments. Leaning close to her from where he sat adjacent to her at the small table, he slid his palm over the bare skin of her thigh, to where the high hem of her skirt ended.

"Yeah," she whispered breathily, biting her lower lip as heat spread across her at his touch.

"Well, you make me want to be the best I can be, Val. For you. Always," he said softly, his voice low. He was so handsome in a

143

DANIELLE BAKER

button down, short sleeved shirt, the pale blue a stunning contrast to his dark coloring. The muscles of his shoulders and arms pulled at the material, and his tattoos were extra visible with the short sleeves straining around his biceps. Despite the heat of the day, he wore a pair of jeans and a pair of black boots. "I'm just glad I wasn't the idiot that let you get away."

His fingers curled around the inside of her left thigh, sandwiched between her legs, his thumb stroking over the smooth skin there, making her entire body hum with need. "Beau..."

"Hmm?" he asked innocently, still leaning close. His dark eyes sparkled with mischief. Oh, he knew exactly what he was doing. A few more inches up, and his fingers would know just how wet she was. Not that it ever took much. He was too sexy for her own good. She was in a perpetual state of arousal.

Two men stopped at their table and Val shifted slightly, her cheeks flaring red when their eyes drifted down to where Beau's hand was situated between her thighs, halfway beneath her short skirt. He squeezed the meaty part of her leg, but didn't pull his hand away, instead letting his thumb continue its lazy strumming along her skin.

"Beau, Val, how was everything tonight?" Grant Price asked. He wore a crisp white button-down shirt, the sleeves rolled up to reveal his forearms, and the top two buttons were left undone in deference to the heat outside. His dark hair was brushed back from his forehead.

"Everything was wonderful, as usual," Val said with a smile, covering Beau's hand with her own and squeezing his fingers. "Van, that Caesar salad with the lemon salmon was incredible. I could have licked my plate."

The tall blonde laughed, revealing a stunningly attractive smile. His white chef jacket was pristine and wrinkle free; she didn't know how he did it. When she cooked, she ended up with a mess to rival an explosion. His jacket sleeves were also rolled to his forearms, and she was surprised to see them covered in

144

tattoos. "Thank you, Val. It's one of our simpler dishes, but definitely a favorite. Very light for hot days like today."

"We had hoped to see you before we head out of town," Grant said, and then waved to a waiter. The waiter stepped forward, setting a beautiful dessert between herself and Beau.

"Rose Blossom Panna Cotta Tart," Van said, gesturing to the dessert. "We're just glad we were a part of your origin story. Happy six months to you; we look forward to being a part of many more of your milestones."

"This is beautiful," Val said, stunned. Picking up one of the forks, she passed it to Beau before picking up her own and slicing into the delicate dessert. After tasting it, she rolled her eyes. "This isn't fair. Can we hire you to cook for us all the time?"

"We can't afford him," Beau chuckled, and Van grinned. Glancing up at the two men, he asked, "You said you're going out of town?"

"We were invited to a food expo in Chicago this weekend, so we will be gone for several days," Grant said and shook his head, shoving his hands into the front pockets of his navy slacks. Nodding toward Van, he laughed, "I'll have a tough time hauling him back. He lives for this shit. Pardon my language."

"Well good luck and have a great time! We'll be sure to come check out anything new you decide to try after you get back," Val said and grinned. "I'll be a willing test subject any day, just say the word."

"Thank you, and you two have a great evening. I'm sure we will see you back soon," Van said and laughed, then the two walked back toward the doors leading into the restaurant.

Beau's fingers squeezed her thigh again and she stifled a moan when his pinkie drifted over the lace that covered her sex. She bit her lip and raised her eyes to look at him. His eyes were dark, burning with intensity. Whispering, she said, "Beau. Please."

He grinned, his white teeth flashing in contrast to the darkness of his beard, and the sexiness of it made her belly flutter.

Damn he's so handsome. And mine, she thought dazedly. *Only mine.*

Leaning close, he kissed her, sending his tongue spiraling into her mouth, only lifting when she was breathless and trembling. "You know I can never say no when you ask, my sweet Valentina."

**Coming Soon to the
Holiday Novella Collection!**
Birthday Wishes featuring Grant, Van, and Hope in a delicious and decadent why choose, curvy fmc, secret identity, spicy romance novella!

ABOUT THE AUTHOR

Danielle Baker, romance author of the *Petoskey Stone Series*, including *Love Unbound, Best Kept Secrets*, and *A Heart So Wild*, was born and raised in the beautiful city of Petoskey, nestled on the crystalline shores of Lake Michigan. She is married to the love of her life, Nicholas, and they have four children between them. Danielle's love of writing began while she was in high school. She wrote a slew of short stories and had written three novels by the time she graduated. Life got busy and writing was put on hold for many years while she started her family. At the urging of her mother, sister, and husband, Danielle was given the boost she needed to "get back in the saddle" and keep reaching for her life-long dream of becoming a published author. When Danielle isn't working, writing, or spending time with her family, she can be found with a cup of coffee in one hand and a book in the other.

ACKNOWLEDGMENTS

I truly cannot believe that we are here at the end of my fourth book, and the first in my newest series! What an adventure this has been, and I truly feel so blessed to be doing what I love! Thank you all for your continued love and support throughout this journey!

Mom, you were my first and always my biggest fan, and the best proofreader around. Without your love and support this wouldn't have been possible! You knew when I was fifteen that I would be here one day, even when I doubted it myself. On to book FIVE already with so many others on the way! I love you!

Nick my love, thank you for letting me hide away at my desk for hours—and sometimes days—on end. Thank you for messaging me that my breakfast, lunch, or dinner was waiting for me when I was ready for it, because you knew I wouldn't even think about eating (thank you, Chef). Thank you for your unwavering support, faith, and enthusiasm for this passion of mine. Without you and the love you give me, I wouldn't have started writing again. Without your support, I wouldn't be able to do this full-time. You are my biggest cheerleader, my love. You are my forever Prince Charming. I love you!

Kara, you have been such a champion in my corner, for your unwavering faith in these stories and in me! And THANK YOU for excitedly and willingly volunteering as tribute to come with me to all our author events! I can't wait to see what kind of trouble we can get into!

Haley, KG, Ava, and Melanie; Thank you to these wonderful fellow authors that I have had the pleasure of being on this journey with! Haley, thank you for always being a critical and willing sounding board, and the Tessa to my Jodi! KG, Ava, Melanie, HOLY MOLY, I'm so glad I met you and feel fortunate to be traversing this new journey with you and a million thank you's for taking me under your wings! Thank you, ladies! I can't wait to see you all at future events!

Melody with Aurora Publicity, thank you sooo much for the absolutely gorgeous cover! KG, thank you for always being a willing mentor and saving me in my moment of crisis!

To my **Booktok Baddies**, April and all the wonderful **Smut Sluts**, **The SmutHood**, and Courtney and Dorothy and all the **Michigan Booktok Babes**, THANK YOU for allowing me to be unapologetic in my shameless promotions and all of you that have recommended The *Petoskey Stone Series* to this absolutely voracious world of spicy romance readers! To my amazing **Street Team**, THANK YOU for loving these crazy characters and their stories as much as I do! I hope you all love Val and Beau's story, too! I can't wait to introduce you to Grant, Van, and Hope next in the *Holiday Novella Collection*, as well as Roxy and Travis in the next for the *Petoskey Stone Series*! I love all of you!

To all the people that are not named but have beta read, listened to me venting or joined in my excitement over each new milestone, and all those that have rooted for me in this scary and enthralling journey, thank you! I wouldn't be here without you!

Lastly, to all my readers, old and new, this has only been possible because of the love and support you've shown me and these characters. I hope you love reading their story as much as I've loved writing it. Val and Beau's story literally just fell out of me and onto the page, and I'm so glad they're here! I look forward to introducing you to MANY more in the future! Thank you!

ALSO BY DANIELLE BAKER

Love Unbound

Best Kept Secrets

A Heart So Wild

Upcoming Novels in the Petoskey Stone Series!

When Hearts Collide (Roxy and Travis) coming spring 2024!

Stay With Me (Graham and Thea)

Hard To Love (Tommy and Liv)

That One Night (Fallon and Jace)

New Series beginning February 2024!

Holiday Romance Novella Collection

Be Mine, Valentine (Val and Beau)

Birthday Wishes (Grant, Van, and Hope)

Meet Me Under the Mistletoe (Noelle and Theo)

Lucky In Love (Willow and Reeve)

www.ingramcontent.com/pod-product-compliance
Ingram Content Group UK Ltd.
Pitfield, Milton Keynes, MK11 3LW, UK
UKHW021503270825
7605UKWH00018B/203

9 798988 045663